MR. AND MRS. CUGAT
The Record of a Happy Marriage

MR. AND MRS. CUGAT

The Record of a Happy Marriage

By ISABEL SCOTT RORICK

ILLUSTRATED BY FLOYD A. HARDY

HOUGHTON MIFFLIN COMPANY · BOSTON

The Riverside Press Cambridge

The Riverside Press
CAMBRIDGE · MASSACHUSETTS
PRINTED IN THE U.S.A.

TO
C. H. R.

CONTENTS

...*forsaking all others*...

MR. CUGAT was a little older than Mrs. Cugat, so that there had been a period of several years during which he, full-fledged and out in the world, sportively tried his wings while she still pounded the playing fields of Westover. These years were looked back on by Mr. Cugat, when he looked back, with nostalgic pleasure and some pride; they were recalled by Mrs. Cugat in glum conjecture. When she had finally laid away her hockey stick, emerged, and, at her own début, encountered Mr. Cugat, he was glamorous indeed. He and Cory Cartwright and Howard Sturm and several others, long since grown simple and familiar, were then prevalently known as 'The Drakes' and lived together at a club. They were socially in great demand and amiably obliged at débutante teas, dinners, and balls, but on their own time, it was understood, they were all mixed up with a married crowd — considered fast. Save for

Howie Sturm nearly being named a co-respondent and Cory getting some bad liquor, most of the Drakes came through this entanglement unscathed, to be pathetically routed and dispersed in no time by the verdant charms of Mrs. Cugat's year of débutantes. It was generally felt by ex-Drakes, in wistful reverie, that those were the days, and Drake wives had to hear a good many jocular allusions to this Saturnalian era. In fact, through fond repetition, Drake exploits had acquired an almost epic quality; so it was with an acute sense of shock that Mrs. Cugat suddenly found herself facing legend in the flesh.

'Well, well, Georgie! Guess who's back in town!' Cory, eyes alight, struggled out of his raincoat and strode into the snug quiet of a Monday evening, rubbing his hands pleasurably. 'Myra Ponsonby herself, my boy, more beautiful than ever and bleating for you!' With a confederate's nudge for Mrs. Cugat, he sat down on the couch beside her and stretched out to relish Mr. Cugat's discomposure.

'No!' said Mr. Cugat, unbelieving, and looking not in the least discomposed but on the whole rather pleased. 'Where's *she* been all these years?'

'Setting the capitals of Europe afire, I hear. This last time she married the Salted Peanut King, and they get around. She's never forgotten you, though — in spite of pleasures and palaces; you were the first thing she asked for when she hit town.'

He chortled gleefully, and Mr. Cugat stroked the back of his head and reddened in a pleased way. Mrs. Cugat tried to make up her mind whether to look surprised, which she was, amused, which she wasn't, or just politely questioning, but nothing seemed to fit her face, which felt stiff with dismay.

'She's visiting Peg and Jimmie Paterno again,' Cory went on, bubbling with information. 'They had a party last night at the club that left only the four walls standing. Old man Crossett went out to play golf and found a Virginia ham, three etchings, and somebody's socks on the tenth green this morning. Kitty Dupré's having cocktails tomorrow night and wants you to come. I told her she'd better call Liz.'

'I don't even know her. Does she want me too?' asked Mrs. Cugat in a small voice.

'Oh, sure! Myra can hardly wait to get a look at the gal who finally hooked George!'

That night Mrs. Cugat prayed fervently for an act of God to end all cocktail parties, but it was not forthcoming; Mrs. Dupré called bright and early next morning.

'And I won't take no for an answer,' she said in a compelling voice that dissolved Mrs. Cugat. 'Myra wants to see George (and you too, dear) more than anyone else in town, she says. Those two were dear friends way-back-when — ha! ha!' Mrs. Cugat tittered appreciatively, accepted, and put down the phone with a sigh. Well, she was in for it — and her black-and-gold was at the cleaner's. It looked as though she would have to stand revealed as the gal who finally hooked George in last summer's blue lace, which never had been a success. Life played odious tricks.

Mr. Cugat, when informed of the evening's plans, was enthusiastic. 'Good!' he said. 'That'll be fun — seeing some different people for a change. Wasn't that nice of old Kitty to think of us!' Myra was not mentioned.

'Vanta guide?' inquired Cory that night, sticking his head into the Cugats' Buick as it drew to a stop before a turreted pile of pink stucco.

'For goodness' sake! I always wondered who lived here,' whispered Mrs. Cugat, wide-eyed. 'What's the Dupré business, anyway? They must be *rolling!*'

'They are, darling,' Mr. Cugat said. 'Martin's a dues collector for the union.'

Mrs. Cugat found her eyebrows raised delicately and put them severely back where they belonged. Don't be that way, now, she reminded herself, narrow-minded like some women. The thing to do is to cultivate a man's point of view and enjoy people for what they *are*, like George and Cory do, not criticize them for what they *aren't*. This cosmo-

politan attitude did a good deal to fortify her quail-
ing spirit, but she concluded, in the mirror-lined
powder room where she took off her coat, that it
would be a lot easier to be urbane and charming in
almost anything but old blue lace. Who'd ever
thought of blue lace, anyway, and left it around for
people to buy!

Myra Ponsonby — the Salted Peanut King's
name was Minke, but apparently nobody cared —
was standing against the mantel when Cory Cartwright and Mr. and Mrs. George Cugat from the
right side of the tracks were ushered in. Mrs. Cugat
took one look at Mrs. Minke and wanted to go right
home. She had always had, but never bothered to
verify, a positive mental conception of George's
Myra belonging to the early Clara Bow period.
Here she stood in person, looking very much as
Mrs. Cugat had always wished she looked herself —
late Hedy Lamarr. Her eyes were deep and smoky,
her lips wide and dark, her hair a swinging bronze
mane; she was nicely turned out in gold lamé and
square emeralds.

'Well, George!' she said as Mrs. Cugat went down
for the count of ten, 'this *is* nice!' Her voice was
sweet and, of course, husky. It would be.

The party caught, momentarily, in an eddy of
greetings and introductions, but then surged on
again unpent, and Mrs. Cugat found herself borne

out into the current unfamiliarly supported by an Old-Fashioned made out of Scotch and Mr. Minke. Mr. Minke, however, proved somewhat of a comfort. He thought Mrs. Cugat was cute, and said so. The fact that nothing Mr. Minke said seemed to carry any weight at all with the rest of the party divested this conquest of any triumph, but she was grateful to him — a mistake, as it turned out.

Platoons of drinks appeared and disappeared — most of them rare mongrels like Mrs. Cugat's Old-Fashioned. One had no feeling of security, she thought, drinking out in the unknown, this way. Ten o'clock came and went, but the subject of dinner was not brought up. Mr. Cugat and Myra were together on a couch, surrounded by admiring members of the Old Guard. Everything either of them said was greeted by salvos. Mrs. Cugat couldn't hear any of it, but as she watched them out of the tail of her eye, a once familiar feeling of awe began to steal over her. Mr. Cugat *was* attractive! She'd just grown so used to him, she'd forgotten. She looked again and he shone with new mystery. Her last drink, a pink one, welled emotionally inside her. By now, it was probably too late for amends. Cory, in the next room, also with a large following, was doing an old specialty, a sort of decadent hula. At her feet, with wistfully upturned eyes, Mr. Minke bared his soul — Myra, of course, did not understand him and was a bitch, but withal too good for him. The story of how he came to be King of Salted Peanuts impended.

Interminable as this all looked to be, however, the hostess put an abrupt end to it by suddenly announcing that she was plastered. Kitty? Old Hollow Leg? Go on! Maybe she needed a little food. How about a little food? The suggestion was seized upon rapturously, but unfortunately for old Hollow Leg, who quietly passed out in the interim, it was a good hour before The Wigwam, a roadhouse thirty miles out on the lake shore, was finally decided upon.

Mrs. Cugat found herself driving there alone with the Salted Peanut King, whom, by now, she called Marko; but, she admitted, she had only herself to blame. There had been a general understanding, very apparent but tactfully unexpressed, that Mr. Cugat and his Myra would want to be alone, and so they were now together in the Minke Bugatti roadster. Mr. Cugat had appeared a little surprised at this arrangement and had sought Mrs. Cugat's eyes over the heads of the crowd, but she had perversely avoided them and announced that she and Marko would go together in *her* car and, to make a good job of it, even archly intimated that they had hoped for just this arrangement. At this Marko had been so manifestly delighted that Cory had looked anxious. Mrs. Cugat now knew why. She had made the last twenty miles by driving with her left, covering with her right, and keeping her elbow in Marko's stomach.

'What's the matter with you, honey?' he grumbled, temporarily subdued by a quick one to the shins. 'I just don't get it.'

'Never mind,' she muttered, stepping hard on the accelerator. 'We all make mistakes.'

'Think of old Myra and her fella,' he remarked wistfully after a time; and then in admiration, 'She's no cold turnip!' Mrs. Cugat chilled further with anxiety. She'd probably never see George again. Mr. Cugat and Mrs. Minke, however, were discovered eating frog-legs at The Wigwam, looking unperturbed and immaculate.

'What you need, child, is a pick-up,' said Cory solicitously, as she drooped in relief at the dining-room door.

'Also a rubdown,' she snapped, and made wearily for the dressing-room.

She felt a little better after she'd had dinner, but not much. The food was delicious and the music and entertainment excellent; also Marko had vanished and she found herself being looked after by Mr. Martin Dupré, Treas., who seemed rather a dear. But, she thought, simmering with indignation, how could she enjoy anybody or anything with Mr. Cugat being stolen away right under her nose? And, obviously, she was losing him. True, he had waved when she came in and said, 'OK, Liz?' with a familiar expression, but had irresponsibly gone off to dance as soon as she'd smiled in brave reassurance. The louse, she sniffed miserably. How could he just forget her this way after all their years together? But she could see how. Myra, obviously, brought out the real George Cugat, the brilliant George. Sitting there beside him, casual and lovely, she was spurring him to unprecedented heights. Right now, he was being funny. 'Tell your old favorite, George, about the twins in the sleeping-car,' someone cried, between paroxysms, and off he went into a story Mrs. Cugat had never heard before in her life.

When the dancing began again, the people at the other tables turned to watch. Myra, always spectacular, with her eyes closed was breath-taking. Dancing with Mr. Cugat she kept them closed. Mr. Cugat swirled and dipped, absorbed and expert. Mrs. Cugat, dancing with Martin Dupré, who was jolly and liked to rhumba, had to avert her own eyes from them in wretchedness.

He cut in on her presently, humming happily. 'Having fun, sweet?' he asked, but before she could swallow the lump in her throat to answer, somebody else cut in on him. Probably just as well, she thought; she might have burst into tears.

'Let's go into the bar,' she said recklessly to her new partner. 'I want another of those pink things.'

Her new partner was Mr. Spinelli, who owned The Wigwam. 'Don't drink that slop, girlie,' he begged, with feeling. 'Let me get you some of my own stuff.' She thanked him, comforted — somebody cared.

Feeling rather special and considerably bolstered (Mr. Spinelli's own stuff, Otard, 1848), she returned to the table to find Mr. Cugat and Myra being urged to sing. They had sung divinely together in the old days, several people whispered to her aside. Mr. Cugat said modestly that he hadn't sung in years and didn't know the words to anything new, which brought down a storm of incredulity. He didn't mean to sit there and tell them that he was

just letting that voice of his get rusty and go to waste! The pity of it ——

'Don't you and Elizabeth ever sing together, Geordo?' Myra asked gently. Mrs. Cugat, who couldn't carry the air of 'Yankee Doodle,' felt her stock plunge again.

'Not if he can help it!' she put in lightly, in what she hoped was an amused tone. Everybody just looked sorry. So he and Myra did a couple of old ones to cheer them up — 'Do, Do, Do What You Done, Done, Done Before, Baby,' with gestures, and a crooning arrangement of 'Moonlight on the Ganges,' with their heads close together. Both were greeted with cheers, and the orchestra leader came over and urged them to come up to the mike. But Mrs. Minke, looking no less radiant, seemed suddenly spent.

'Darling,' she said to Mr. Cugat, 'I'm tired and I'm tight — take me home.'

'Where's Marko?' asked Mr. Cugat.

'In bed with the help again, I suppose — the poor goon's so oversexed.' She came around the table to Martin Dupré. 'Geordo and I want to go riding in the woods tomorrow, Marty,' she said, resting a lovely hand on the back of Mr. Dupré's neck, 'but he says all his breeches got eaten by moths. Can I bring him up to the house after lunch and put a pair of yours on him?'

Mrs. Cugat ground her teeth. She might have
known, of course — Geordo, with marriage, had also
given up horses. 'Polo! With a wife to support?' he
was wont to say. She'd heard that one before. Still,
from loyalty, he might have omitted that moth story.

'You don't mind, do you?' said Mrs. Minke unexpectedly, looking at Mrs. Cugat for, apparently, the
very first time.

'Not at all,' Mrs. Cugat replied politely, and
couldn't seem to think of anything more.

Mr. Cugat rose, tossed the Minke sables over his
arm, shook hands with his host, clapped the orchestra leader on the back, and made easy and unruffled
adieus. As he passed Mrs. Cugat's chair, he said
cheerfully: 'Collect Cory when you come, will you?
He's in the gambling-room.' Everybody waved a
farewell of tender understanding.

The party went on into what seemed eternity.
'I'll stay until the end if it lasts until day after to-
morrow,' she vowed to herself, grimly sipping Mr.
Spinelli's brandy. 'Nobody's going to think I care.'

She drove home in the dim dawn and left Cory
snoring in the garage. Mr. Cugat, rather to her
surprise, was tucked safe in his bed and looked entirely natural. The windows were opened a foot at
the bottom and a foot at the top in his accustomed
manner and the curtains were carefully looped aside.
The alarm clock ticked briskly on the table beside

him, correctly set for seven-thirty, and he had rather touchingly left the lamp on. Nothing seemed to point to an emotional crisis in his life — but you couldn't tell about men, they took things differently. She shivered out of her clothes in the bathroom and noted that one of the towels had lipstick on it. Was it hers or Myra's? She was too miserable to care.

It was well past noon when she awakened, weak and peaked. Just about now, she mused, staring desolately at the alarm clock, he and that woman would be lingering over their lunch — or were they already out at the Duprés' pink palace intimately involved in changing Mr. Cugat's pants? Mr. Cugat hadn't been on a horse since the Governor's funeral, she reflected with some pleasure, and he hadn't been any too firm then. But he looked lovely in riding-breeches — almost dashing. Damn!

Anna arrived bearing coffee; she had, she said, been up since five. Mr. Cartwright, at that time, had thrown a wrench through her window and asked her if she would call him a cab. Then he'd gone to sleep on the front steps waiting for it to come and she and the driver had had a time waking him up again. She couldn't say what the neighbors were thinking. A drinking man, she concluded, was a sorrow.

Mrs. Cugat presented her with the blue lace and applied herself to the coffee. By the time she'd had some aspirin and a shower, her mood had changed from despair to wrath. Imagine George, *her* George, out there, all booted and spurred and idling along a bridle path with that middle-aged glamour-girl! A desire to hit something hard grew so strong that she sensibly decided on nine holes of golf. She wondered what La Minke's golf was like. She was indubitably 'superb' on a horse — just that leggy type.

It was a lovely day — warm sun and soft air. Dispensing with her caddy, she resolutely shouldered her bag and started down the hill after her first drive; sped by ire, it had almost caught up with a foursome of men playing their approach shots. She plodded rapidly along with her head down and, reaching her ball, looked up to find the foursome still on the green.

'Hurry up, hurry up,' she muttered irritably, shading her eyes — and then her bag slid from her limp hand. She shut her eyes and opened them again. What had happened! That nearly knee-length tan sweater and that oddly decrepit putting stance could belong to no other. There was Mr. Cugat!

His ball dropped neatly into the cup and he turned to look as she hurried toward them.

'Hi, there,' he called. 'How do *you* feel?'

'I'm all right,' she gulped dazedly.

'Cory isn't,' said Mr. Cugat, happily prodding his partner. 'We've brought him out to put roses back in those cheeks, haven't we, Tank?'

'But George,' said Mrs. Cugat uncertainly, 'I thought you were going riding, in the woods, with Myra ——'

Mr. Cugat's face did not change —not for a full minute; then all expression left it. 'Oh-oh,' he breathed softly, 'I forgot!'

Mr. Cugat had forgotten things before. Mrs. Cugat knew all the authentic signs — that still tone, that empty look. Rapture enveloped her. 'But darling,' she said, nearly breathless with it, 'that's awful. She must have waited and waited ——'

'What'll I do?' asked Mr. Cugat.

'It's not too late,' she said, with some nobility. 'Go into the club and call her.'

'Oh, Liz, *no* — ! Hell, we've been trying to get this foursome together for weeks — all my bets are honeys. Can't we fix it some way? You can always cook up a good story — that's just your stuff. Tell her something, won't you?'

'Well,' said Mrs. Cugat, 'I might.'

Care fell visibly from his shoulders and he patted her gratefully on the head. 'Atta girl!' he said, starting blithely off toward the second tee. 'Make it good, but — you know, not *too* fancy!'

Cory dropped back a step. 'And wipe that grin off your face,' he murmured behind his hand. 'Do you want to *blind* people?'

...*for better, for worse*...

IN THE city in which Mr. and Mrs. Cugat lived, the peak of the social season was glitteringly crowned by a function called the Bal Masqué of the Coronet. It was *the* party of the year, and had been considered so ever since its ceremonial beginnings back in the stately eighties. Gilded with tradition and bristling with solemn and complicated customs, its invitations or lack of them made and broke strong men. Dowagers (staggered with a careful eye to precedence) reigned from tiered, bunting-draped boxes; débutante queens were crowned with pearls; masked dignitaries awarded prizes for beauty and originality and the orchestra was imported from New York. If you had met in your travels any people of importance to whom you had said, 'You must come and visit us!' you always had them, if you could get them, for the Coronet Ball, so that the assemblage was always, not only large, but cosmopolitan and illustrious.

This year the invitations had artily proclaimed, on a sheet of supposed papyrus, that The Secret Committee of the Coronet commanded your presence on Saturday, November twentieth, at 'Un Bal Afrique' — the papyrus, to give you a general idea, being thoughtfully decorated with a three-color sphinx, palm tree, and Bedouin. Costumes were always a matter for grave debate, and the usual public discussion and private agonizing over them had been rife for a month, but as it was now half-past five of the afternoon of the momentous day it could be assumed that all were at last in readiness.

It could be assumed so, but the assumption would be wrong. Mr. Cugat was not ready — by any means. He was personally conducting, on a tour of the city's major industries, the president of the bank in which he worked and a high official of the Bank of England, and his costume, always apt to be a last-minute affair, had slipped his mind entirely.

The high official and his wife had been encountered by Mr. Cugat's bank's president and his wife on shipboard, and duly asked to visit for the Coronet Ball. They had accepted and turned up (being English), and much of the responsibility of presenting the keys to the city had fallen to Mr. Cugat, who, while but a third vice-president and ostensibly just along to open doors, was crown prince in the line of succession at his bank, and liable. Not only did he

have to tour the city on the day of the Ball, but,
standing staunchly by his superior, he had under-
taken to entertain the Bank of England at Sunday
lunch the day after the Ball; so that, with one thing
and another, it was no wonder that a costume was
not among his worries.

It was among Mrs. Cugat's, though, who was at
home marshaling forces to get the silver cleaned
against the morrow and compiling warning lists of
familiar pitfalls for Anna, the cook. Mrs. Cugat
loved costumes, and had had her own ready on the
guest-room bed for a week. If only he would let her
get his! But Mr. Cugat, when helpfully approached,
always declined aid and said he'd rather see to his
own. Which meant that he and Cory Cartwright
and that Bill Stone usually ended up by renting The
Three Musketeers from a filthy place downtown
(happily oblivious to whether it was a Cruise Ball or
a Surrealist Pageant) and spending an inseparable
evening saying 'All for one and one for all!'

'Be sure the toast for the chicken hash is crisp,
Anna,' she said, counting out fruit knives auto-
matically, 'and make the coffee fresh and strong.'
Five-thirty! He ought to be getting home ——
If he had forgotten his costume again, she might
fix him up in a turban and let him wear his dress
suit. Or was it in India that they wore turbans?
Should she use her Pointe de Venice runner on the

bare table tomorrow or her new silk damask cloth? She ought really to try them both, right now, to see which was best, but, unless she wanted to look like a hag for the Ball, she'd better call it a day and take a bath and a quick nap. 'Remember those bottles of hock in the pantry, Anna; don't put them on ice until late tomorrow morning. I'm going to bathe now, but I want to be called if Mr. Cugat phones.'

Mr. Cugat phoned the moment she got into the tub. 'I just got back to the office,' he said in a weary tone. 'We covered the whole damned town. What are the plans?'

'We're supposed to be at the Sturms' for cocktails and sandwiches at seven-thirty and to go on to the Ball from there. What have you done about a costume?'

Having done nothing, he was appalled for the moment. 'Good Lord, that's right ——' Then he said easily: 'I'll tell you. It's so late, why don't you call Cory and have him pick you up? I'll go down to Nemo's and get into some rig and meet you at the Sturms'.'

She protested vigorously, having no faith in Nemo's rigs. But he finally won her over — his mail hadn't been signed yet, it would take him an extra half-hour to come way out home. 'Don't you worry; Nemo always fixes me up fine,' he said. So she acceded reluctantly. Anyway, this time he couldn't be a musketeer.

She called Cory and began to dress, forgetting, as her enthusiasm mounted, some of her doubts and weariness. She was going to look very nice. Miss Terry had done extremely well with *her* costume. It was an Arab dancer's. Around the waist, however, the skirt and bolero did not meet, but left about two inches of bare diaphragm. Would the Bank of England, she wondered, consider this entirely proper for the wife of a third vice-president? It was hard to tell about the English: the ones one met always seemed to be either ten times as broad-minded as Americans or twenty times as stuffy. No middle-path people. Prudently, she added a pink silk undershirt. No use jeopardizing Mr. Cugat's day's work.

Cory, duly arriving, was accompanied by the reprehensible Mr. Stone, whom nobody had seen or heard of since the last Coronet. They were dressed in uniforms of the Foreign Legion, and inordinately pleased with themselves for having thought to fill their two quart canteens with Scotch. Mrs. Cugat offered a silent prayer of thanksgiving for what Mr. Cugat had just missed.

'You look like a million dollars, baby,' said Cory. 'What's George going to do, revert to type and go as a sheik?'

'Oh, Cory, I don't know! He's been so tied up, he never thought of his costume until half an hour ago. He's going down to that Nemo place and pick up something there.'

'Nemo hasn't much left,' said Cory thoughtfully. 'Most of his stuff would crawl away if you opened the door. Bill and I had ours cleaned, but they still have a funny smell. Do you notice it?'

She did, but politely denied it, so they proceeded to the Sturms' after a solemn round of dusty Scotch from the canteens to quell that usual last-minute fear that perhaps, inexplicably, nobody else would be in costume.

Everybody was, however, and the party well under way. They went in, feeling much better from the Scotch, and were acclaimed. Mrs. Cugat was implored by all to discard the undershirt, but she managed to remain steadfast to her sober decision and kept it on.

It was not until an hour later, while she was sitting on the stair-landing beginning to wonder about Mr. Cugat, that her companion, a Riff bandit from New York, looked down and exclaimed, 'Why, girls, here comes the Prince!'

The Prince was coming in rather clumsily and spectacularly attired — in a full suit of armor. What had doubtless been described in its prime as 'mighty armor'; a cast-off, perhaps, of Sir Gawain, whose strength was as the strength of ten. Of somebody, at any rate, whose strength was considerably superior to that of Prince Cugat, who was looking very small and tired to death. He gave an impression of not so much wearing his armor as of cozily living in it, probably along with a bed and a couple of chairs. His eyes just came up to the little latticed peek-hole in the visor, and he peered out with effort like a man standing on tiptoe to see over a high windowsill.

Mrs. Cugat rushed down to his side while he creakily greeted his hostess amid a gathering throng. 'Well, George!' — 'Where have you been, boy?' — 'How perfectly darling — so African!' — 'Get a can-opener and we'll give him a drink!'

'Give me two drinks,' said Mr. Cugat exhaustedly.

'Poor old Georgie! Come out in the dining-room and catch up with the party.'

'Hello, Liz,' he said soberly as he passed Mrs. Cugat. 'This is the best I could do.' He was borne off to the dining-room.

'Quite a card,' observed the Riff briefly, as she rejoined him on the stairs.

The cocktail party went on and on. The Cugats' set had seen plenty of Coronet Balls — there was no need to hurry. Just so they got there before the Queen was crowned. Mrs. Cugat was still sitting on the landing with the Riff when the first move was made to go. 'I'd better look up George,' she said, getting up. But just then Mr. Cugat appeared below, with him his good friend Mr. Stone. 'The greatest and best friend a man ever had,' as he was telling the Legionnaire at that moment. The two of them started up the stairs with resolve and not without some difficulty. Mrs. Cugat, looking down, met a disturbing realization: Mr. Cugat had caught up. And he had not just drawn well to the fore, he was away out in front.

'Are you the guy who called me a prince?' he demanded abruptly, swinging his leg heavily over the last step and clanking up to the Riff.

'Run along, Cup-cake, you're tight,' that person retorted in high good humor.

Surprised, momentarily, by the stunning indignity of being called a cup-cake, Mr. Cugat had to wait a minute before he could reply. 'Say that again,' he finally managed with menace. The Riff languidly turned his back. 'Afraid, eh, Emily?' said Mr. Cugat, triumphantly moving around in front of his quarry. Mrs. Cugat averted her eyes and prayed.

'Oh, go away,' said the Riff, and gave him a light, impatient push on the chest. It could hardly have been called a push at all, and would scarcely have resulted as such if Mr. Cugat had not been standing on a landing dressed in armor. As it was, he tottered back a step, caught his eight-inch spurs in the railing and plunged sideways down the stairs, sounding like a load of tin cans cascaded down a chute.

A moment of awful silence ensued, followed by shrieks and concerned exclamations, and the hall filled. 'Take off his helmet!' — 'Are you hurt, old boy?' — 'Where does he undo?' Mrs. Cugat glared at the Riff, who looked considerably concerned, resisted an urge to slap him, and sped down the stairs. Mr. Cugat was being helped tenderly to his feet, several pairs of hands tugging helpfully at the helmet. 'How do you get this thing off?' — 'It's jammed or something ——'

'How are you, George, all right?' Mr. Stone called through a crack, anguished. Mr. Cugat remained silent, but with sudden vigor made an aborted attempt to charge back up the stairs again. Cory pushed through to his side. 'Listen, George, we'd better take this thing off,' he said soothingly, investigating the helmet situation anew. But it would not come off — it was jammed and badly bent. Mr. Cugat, after submitting to considerable impotent wrenching and hammering, suddenly decided to close the incident. Brushing off his sympathizers, he walked determinedly out the front door, arm-linked with his good friend Mr. Stone, and was seen no more.

'Cory,' groaned Mrs. Cugat miserably, climbing into his car, 'what will we *do* about him? To get tight tonight — of all nights! Mr. Atterbury and the Bank of England will surely see him, and tomorrow we have to have them to lunch. What a pleasant meal that will be!'

'He and Bill did get their noses a little wet,' Cory replied temperately, 'but don't you worry about old George. He can handle himself, every time!'

'He isn't doing a very outstanding job so far,' she replied sententiously.

'Well, but look — that Great Big Beautiful Thing pushed him! By God! When I think of a twirp like that pushing George ——'

'He didn't have to push very hard,' Mrs. Cugat replied soberly, in all fairness; 'and besides, George wanted to fight. It isn't a bit like him, is it? Usually, drinking makes him so agreeable he'd let his worst enemy walk on his face. I'll bet that damned Stone

man put him up to it — he's always causing
trouble!'

'Now, Liz, Bill Stone's one of the best. If you
girls only saw more of him ——'

'Thank you, no. If we saw any more of him, we'd
have him ridden out of town on a rail. Here we are
— I'm scared to go in, Cory. Do you suppose
they're here?'

'Probably not. I should think they've most likely
gone down to Nemo's to get that suit off. He'll have
to use a blow torch.'

This surmise appeared correct. Mr. Cugat was
nowhere in sight. The ballroom had been darkened
and the orchestra was playing the prelude to the
processional. They were just in time for the coronation. Mrs. Cugat, with Cory loyally pinch-hitting,
hastened to the Atterbury box, which, being designed for the illustrious, commanded an excellent
and unobstructed view.

'Ah, there you are, my dear,' Mrs. Atterbury
whispered graciously. 'Lady Willington, Mrs. Cugat
— George's wife, you know. And Sir Bercy. Where
is George, Mary Elizabeth?'

'He isn't here yet,' Mrs. Cugat whispered and
summoned all her poise to produce Cory instead,
but just then trumpets pealed out and the lights
went off, a single white spot cutting through to an
impressively curtained doorway at the far end of the

room. Through these portals the Queen was due to
come, the secret of her identity, until this moment,
having been guarded with lives. The trumpets
again pealed, the curtains rippled, and every eye
in the place was trained expectantly on the door.
But nothing happened. Suddenly Mrs. Cugat, who
had let her eyes wander to the galleries in anxious
search, felt Cory stiffen and looked back. A mailed
fist projected awkwardly between the velvet folds.
Wide-eyed, she turned to Cory as he turned to look
at her; then they grasped hands and sent their eyes
doggedly back. Somewhat questioningly, the trumpets pealed again, and this time the curtains bil-
lowed to emit Mr. Cugat.

He appeared totally unaware of the spotlight and
fanfare — shut away and absorbed in a little world
of his own. Casually he sauntered over, still full in
the spot, to a garlanded pillar, and with a good deal
of difficulty, covering perhaps two full minutes,
managed to light himself a cigarette — nine hundred
pairs of eyes watching his faceless fumblings in
fascination. Finally lit, the cigarette preternaturally
disappeared into the helmet and was seen no more,
but its smoke continued to curl tranquilly out the
empty aperture as from a lazy volcano. Composing
himself comfortably, he sank into introspection.

The trumpets blared agitatedly. But now, at
last, the curtains majestically swung aside and the

procession emerged. It was headed by four small page boys, whose round eyes, as they came out into the light, immediately caught Mr. Cugat and remained captivated. And their lagging footsteps carrying them finally past him, they began walking backward. Gorgeously caparisoned handmaidens came next — each with a sidelong glance for the pillar — all in the grip of giggles. Then the music swelled and the Queen appeared, tall, stately, and adorned, and just who everyone knew it would be — only her face was redder than expected. Mr. Cugat remained immobile against his pillar and the tension in the audience slightly relaxed. As the main part of the procession passed him, however, he roused himself abruptly, shook off abstraction, and casually joined the marchers. He did not, however, march. He sauntered leisurely in and out among them, like a man taking a stroll on the Boardwalk amid the Sunday crowds. This caused considerable trouble, as he could apparently see only a very small area directly in front of him; so that, as he wandered along, smoke drifting lazily from his head, he collided severely with one or two maidens and tripped up a masked patriarch who was having plenty of trouble seeing for himself. For a little time he walked companionably beside the Queen, but then, captiously, decided on a left turn. Inasmuch as he was unaware of her, he crossed directly under her chin, so that she was forced to stop dead and this caused a bad pile-up in the rear guard.

Further confusion marked the arrival at the throne — an attendant there making an ill-advised attempt to persuade Mr. Cugat out of the picture and Mr. Cugat, affronted, retaliating with a mailed right to the face. Page boys, handmaidens, and patriarchs, due to arrange themselves with measured tread on appointed chalk marks, broke ranks and gathered round to watch. The Queen, however, apparently done in by the vicissitudes of the march, proceeded on to the throne without bothering even to look, and sank gratefully to her knees to await the crown alone. Mr. Cugat, finishing off the attendant, joined her there. He sat heavily down on the steps at her side, dusted off his hands, stretched his legs out wearily, and then decided, by way of more complete relaxation, to take off his helmet.

Every eye in the hall shone expectantly. Every eye, that is, except Cory's and Mrs. Cugat's. Theirs were shut. But the helmet held, obstinately refusing to divulge its secret, and another crisis passed. The distracted retinue proceeded then to arrange itself hastily and The Secret Committee filed apprehensively out, bearing aloft the crown of pearls. Finally arranged, it was an impressive tableau, and Mr. Cugat, in his shining armor, would have done nothing, really, to mar the medieval pageantry of it, if he had not been lolling so informally and, now, smoking from every crack. He looked like a busy switch engine, paused for respite on a siding.

'Hear ye! Hear ye!' rumbled the head committee-man, sonorously breaking the silence and startling Mr. Cugat, who turned resentfully to stare. Turning far enough around for a successful stare involved considerable personal rearrangement, and he was busy with this as the committeeman continued, pitting his voice against the clanking. 'All those here present on this twentieth day of the eleventh month' — smoke curled around the dignitary's head and he stopped to cough — 'of the year nineteen hundred and forty' — Mr. Cugat here decided to cross his legs and settle down resignedly to listen — 'are solemnly called upon to bear witness ——' But something went wrong; as he lifted it, the leg suddenly twisted convulsively in the air, stiffened out, threw him on his back, and slid him to the bottom of the steps, where he lay, the other leg flailing the floor like a dragon's tail. The voice of the committeeman died away and everyone stood motionless, staring in horrified fascination. It looked like a fit. Then, from a completely prone position, he made a prodigious leap to his feet, leaped again, landed sitting, and started spinning frenziedly around on his rear.

'My God!' shouted Cory suddenly, from the Atterbury box, 'he's on fire!'

The confusion attendant on putting Mr. Cugat
out was terrific. Women screamed and men shouted
and everybody ran to and fro. Somebody tore
down the velvet curtains and somebody else put in
an alarm. The orchestra, in the manner of those on
sinking ships, struck up an inspirational air. Mr.
Cugat, belching smoke, continued to bounce and
writhe on the steps of the throne until a bartender,
with the habitual calm of his profession, ran in and
squirted seltzer into the inviolate helmet. Cheers
and applause rose, but at the height of the tumult a
small, self-possessed cortège surrounded the still
smoldering heap and discreetly vanished with it,
leaving the fifty-second Bal Masqué of the Coronet
to weather a severe anticlimax.

At a quarter of one the next day, per schedule, the president of the Tri-State Trust, Mr. J. Duncan Atterbury, and his wife, accompanied by their guests Sir Bercy and Lady Willington of London, Fettercairn, and Mold, drew up at the door of the Cugat domicile for luncheon. Mrs. Cugat, very pale, but smiling bravely over an elaborate shoulder display of orchids, welcomed them at the door. The orchids, which had arrived only a moment ahead of the Atterburys and Willingtons, were adding immeasurably to her courage. They were from the Riff and had an accompanying note reading, 'After the divorce call WIckersham 2-3486.' Mr. Cugat, in an immaculate morning coat, stood behind her also smiling — through tautened jaws. He too had just been delivered — not a moment before — by his good friend Mr. Stone, to whom, for once, Mrs. Cugat gave full marks. Mr. Cugat's tie and trousers were not precisely what she herself would have chosen — they were both rather vividly striped — and there bloomed upon his lapel a white carnation made of feathers which gave him a dressy church-wedding look. Also he reeked, in an unnatural, man-about-town way, of the barber shop; but he was presentable and *there* — which was all that mattered for the present.

'Well, George,' said Mr. Atterbury heartily, accepting a glass of sherry from Mrs. Cugat's mother's butler, 'where were you last night? We never saw you all evening!' Mrs. Cugat stopped what she was saying and looked quickly at her husband, standing carefully against the mantel. His eyes were fixed and his expression grimly determined. That he was about to do *and* die was evident. Mr. Cugat always had had a foolhardy tendency to face the music, and he was obviously getting ready to do it now. He would make an abject apology, a harrowing clean breast of things, and then probably hand in his resignation. She took a deep breath and plunged.

'George wasn't there,' she said clearly. 'He had a lot of unfinished work, so he just stayed home.' And then, resolutely heading upstream: 'Did you enjoy the party, Lady Willington? I thought it was quite lovely this year — except, of course, for the coronation!' Her laughter rippled out in delicious reminiscence and she turned to Mr. Cugat. 'I didn't get a chance to tell you this morning, George — but the most awful thing happened last night! The coronation was completely disrupted by some ridiculous man in armor who was — well, must have had a few too many. How he got in nobody knows, but he did and barged around and ran into people and finally set himself on fire. The place was in an uproar and the fire department came. They put him out with a seltzer bottle, and nobody,' she finished distinctly, 'knows who he was!'

'It was an outrage!' asserted Mr. Atterbury.

'But damned funny,' put in Sir Bercy, and Mrs. Cugat sprang to refill his glass with her own hands.

'They don't know who he was?' quavered Mr. Cugat in a scratchy voice, starting to sit down and standing again abruptly.

'Nobody has any idea,' she replied firmly, wondering how he was going to manage to sit at lunch. 'Cory came in this morning while you were *down at the office finishing your mail*, and he said that the whole town's wild but nobody knows. The committee are trying to find out, of course' — her tone became slightly vindictive. 'They want to sue.'

'The fool must have come with somebody,' snapped Mr. Atterbury.

'Well, yes,' Mrs. Cugat said judiciously, 'but his own friends would hardly give him away on a serious thing like this, so I don't suppose we'll ever really know.' She paused for breath, wiped her hands on her cocktail napkin, looked up and became again bedewed under Mrs. Atterbury's level gaze from across the room.

'So you stayed home last night like an old fogy, eh?' chided Mr. Atterbury, turning his attention to a more worthy subject and slapping Mr. Cugat's flinching back. 'Don't you know all work and no play makes Jack a dull boy? We can't have that, you know!' Mr. Cugat smiled in sickly apology and Mr. Atterbury continued in indulgent tones: 'If

you don't remind me of myself as a youngster!
Many's the Coronet Ball I passed up because I felt
there were bigger things at stake. But I was wrong
— don't you agree with me, Bercy? Occasional
relaxation is immensely important — immensely.
Doesn't do to keep the nose too close to the grind-
stone! I will say there aren't many around like
George, though, nowadays. Most of the young men
I meet appear to be an irresponsible lot with no
proper regard for anything. Take that fool last
night! By Gad, I'd like to find out who he was.
The fellow ought to be dropped from his clubs!
Such a thing never happened before.'

Mrs. Cugat took her sherry at one gulp and then,
at bay, met Mrs. Atterbury's eyes. That lady's
steady look did not waver, but as Mrs. Cugat resolutely returned her gaze, chin up, Mrs. Atterbury's
lips curled in a reassuring little smile. She turned
to her husband. 'Oh, I don't know, Duncan,' she
said lightly. 'I seem to remember that year Lily
Buchard was Queen, and one of the masked viziers
fell flat on his face and had to be carted out feet
first by two trumpeters.'

Mr. Atterbury choked on his sherry and then
beetled his brows fiercely. '*I* recall no such incident,'
he growled uneasily.

'Possibly one of those Coronets that you passed
up, my dear,' Mrs. Atterbury replied serenely; and
Mrs. Cugat's mother's butler announced lunch.

...in sickness and in health...

LITTLE MRS. CUGAT turned in her bed and blinked lazily at the quiet alarm clock on the table beside her. Half-past eight. Slices of yellow morning sun came through the Venetian blind; coffee flavored the air; a remote hum, off in another part of the house, droned up and down, singing of well-ordered, early vacuum-cleaning. She stretched placidly, reached for a cigarette, and jerked upright. There in the other bed was Mr. Cugat — still there, hunched all up under his covers at eight-thirty.

'Hey!' she cried, swinging her feet out. 'Look at the time!' Mr. Cugat did not move, but his eyes opened slowly — clouded and apathetic.

'I know,' he said with effort, and closed them again.

Alarm washed over her, and she regarded him wide-eyed while she groped for her slippers and got into her bathrobe. 'You aren't going to the office?' she asked uncertainly.

'No,' he replied, eyes still closed. 'I'm sick.'

She bent to feel his head — it was hot. Mr. Cugat hunched deeper into the covers. Hurriedly closing the window, she pattered into the dressing-room and then distractedly out again and into the hall, where she rang urgently for the maid. Mr. Cugat was *never* sick — even the commonest seizures and distempers passed him by; his sinus, duodenum, gall bladder, and appendix were imperturbable; Poisonous Wastes took splendid care of themselves. It seemed appalling that, judging by the look of him, everything had given way at once.

'Anna!' she called, leaning over the stair rail, 'Mr. Cugat isn't feeling well this morning — will you bring up some hot coffee right away!' She hurried back. Mr. Cugat had roused himself and was sitting on the side of his bed, staring at his feet. As she came in, however, he rose and tottered across to the bathroom. 'I'll come down to the dining-room,' he said, and disappeared.

'He says he'll come down, Anna,' she shouted, hurrying back to the banister.

The vacuum-wielder appeared below and tilted up an anxious countenance. 'The dining-room's being cleaned,' she said, wide-eyed.

'Oh. Well, you'll have to bring breakfast up-stairs, then.'

'We only got that one big tray, you know. Can I get everything on it?'

'No — you'll have to set up a card table in the dressing-room.'

'It's Friday.' Dark significance clothed this last.

'I know, Anna, but you'll have to *put off* the cleaning until later. Don't you understand? Mr. Cugat may be dangerously ill!'

'Saints!' said the face and vanished.

Mrs. Cugat returned from the hall and stuck her head in the bathroom door. Mr. Cugat was gargling.

'Shall I call Doctor Buell?' she asked anxiously.

'Maybe you'd better,' he said, spitting without vigor and turning to examine the contents of the medicine cabinet blankly.

She dashed some water on her face in the guest-room bathroom and flew to the phone, colliding in the hall with the approaching card table. The laundress, damp and foreign and obviously wrested from her own pursuits to be hurled into the breach, labored in the table's wake with an abundant tray. Compassionate eyes were bent on Mr. Cugat, who drifted out of the bathroom just then and went to sit miserably on the edge of the window seat in everybody's way. He looked self-conscious and unwanted. Having left word for the doctor, Mrs. Cugat hastened back to his side, love and concern welling up within her. When she reached it, however, she was smitten with unexpected shyness. Mr. Cugat, ill, was a complete stranger. She felt his head again timidly.

Breakfast took some time. It was a cereal morning. Mr. Cugat, toying listlessly with his, said it would be all right with him if they had just boiled eggs always, but never to mind this morning, he wasn't very hungry for anything. Nevertheless, it seemed advisable to start all over and try him with an egg. She shouted down the stair-well again, 'Anna! Mr. Cugat thinks he might like a nice egg ——' and resignedly, the vacuum died away. By the time the egg arrived, however, Mr. Cugat had retired once more behind the bathroom door.

Mrs. Cugat got dressed anxiously, as best she

could without her comb, her powder, or her girdle, which were closeted with Mr. Cugat, and hastened down to rearrange her day. Her hair appointment would have to be canceled; she must get somebody to take her place at the Red Cross Rummage Sale; she must call her mother and tell her *not* to bring Cousin Melba from Cincinnati to tea. She was cold with apprehension, and between phone calls kept running to the living-room windows to see if she could see Doctor Buell. Suffocating pictures of life alone presented themselves. Mr. Cugat's last words — weak but brave. Mr. Cugat in his coffin, with his cutaway on, tucked down into the white satin like candy in a fancy box. Mr. Cugat's pallbearers coming back to the house, the way Tommy Spencer's did, for one last sad drink. Her throat ached.

Mr. Cugat put an end to this by coming downstairs. He had put on a pair of gray flannel trousers over his pyjamas and an old sweater used for duck-hunting; around his neck was his best white silk monogrammed evening scarf, and over all his oldest bathrobe. He shuffled over to the coffee table and sat tentatively down on its edge without saying anything. His hair stuck up and he looked wistful.

'Do you think you ought to be downstairs?' she asked anxiously.

'I don't know, they're doing something to my bed,' he said.

While she was looking into this the doctor came.

Mr. Cugat had a cold. Nothing serious, but he'd better stay home for a day or so and take care of himself. Plenty of rest — stay out of drafts — lots of liquids — two pink tablets alternating with one tan tablet every hour — and gargle with salt water. Mr. Cugat, consoled and interested, sat back in his big chair reviewing his symptoms. Vivacious with relief, Mrs. Cugat saw the doctor to the door and sped upstairs to finish dressing. There was just time to get her hair appointment after all. On her way home she would stop and pick up a detective story and some movie magazines for him. What fun having him home! Darling Mr. Cugat, suddenly vulnerable and inadequate, with his hair sticking up — the Weaker Vessel. Goodness, how she loved him! She could hardly wait to get back downstairs to see if she could do anything to make him more comfortable before she left.

'What about lunch?' Anna caught her at the garage door. 'We planned peanut salad, you know. Will He eat it?'

Of a certainty He would not. 'Ask him what he thinks he'd like, Anna, what sounds *good* to him. I'll be back at one o'clock.'

Laden with two books, three magazines, a pot of tulips, and some white grapes, she came eagerly back up the walk at one to meet Belda, the laundress, resplendent in mufti, emerging from the front door.

'Em goink by da "A" on "P,"' she beamed in explanation.

'The "A and P"?' said Mrs. Cugat. 'What for?'

'Eh nice stek.'

'Why doesn't Anna go?'

'Shiss bissy.'

'Oh —— What else did Mr. Cugat order for lunch?'

'Franch frice ——'

'Ah, yes, of course ——'

'Vechtible soup ——'

'Oh.'

'Shoclit keck — home med. Pore seeck men' — her voice crooned — 'hees hongreh!'

Mrs. Cugat steadied herself. 'And what about the ironing?' she queried.

'Ha! Becawss da fuce — *iss* no ionink!'

'Fuse? What fuse?'

'Da men fuce. Mist Cuga feexis lemps togedda — Zick! da men fuce blos. Now iss no lides — no hut ion. Iss med, da ledy in nomba fife — shess eh cot poddy effta launch now iss no lides in heh house nedda!'

'You mean it blew out hers *too?*'

'Anna sess so.'

Mr. Cugat was discovered in the basement

dispiritedly screwing and unscrewing things — apparently at random. He looked downhearted and was persuaded back upstairs again. In the library she came upon the chain-arrangement of lamps that had been designed to bring light to him over in an obscure corner by the woodbox (out of drafts). His chair was there, and two dismantled shotguns with their cleaning equipment and a highball and the white velvet chaise-longue cover from the guest room.

'Did anyone call an electrician?' she asked, starting to pull things out from where they were and sticking them back where they belonged.

Mr. Cugat lifted absorbed eyes from his new *Film Fun*. 'Yes,' he said, 'but all the electricians are striking today, Anna says. I told her,' he added helpfully, 'that she'd better get some candles.'

Lunch, after all, was disappointing. It was funny, he said, but nothing had any taste. Might as well be eating straw! Surreptitiously Mrs. Cugat, to the best of her capacity, ate for two while Anna was out of the room, but she was obliged to feed most of Mr. Cugat's chocolate cake to Lillian, the cat.

After lunch she went upstairs and got out her knitting. Now they could settle down for the afternoon, cozy and domestic, in front of the fire. She would see that he took his medicine and didn't get bored. Perhaps he'd let her read aloud. Maybe he'd feel like backgammon. How nice — on a cold, dark day like this! When she got back to the library, however, after some delay at the phone (the lights of the people in No. 4 were all *out!* Were the Cugats'?), she found the room empty, the windows open, and the curtains whipping and streaming. Mr. Cugat, at the mercy of the elements and clutching his bathrobe, was out on the balcony, hanging over the rail.

'It's funny about that cat,' he replied, in answer to her squeaks of protest. 'She disappeared like *that!*'

'The cat! Don't tell me you let Lillian out!'

'Only for a minute. She ought to get more exercise — she's getting fat,' he explained reasonably.

'But darling, we *never* let her out alone! She acts like a perfect idiot. Streaks across the street in front of cars and eats garbage and gets up in trees and doesn't know how to get down. Oh, dear! There's not a sign of her. Anybody'd think, with a valuable animal like Lillian, you'd be a little careful. What had I better do, I wonder.'

It seemed sensible that Mrs. Cugat go right out and hunt for Lillian. Mr. Cugat, looking sheepish, came in from the balcony, took a double dose of pills, wrapped his knees tenderly in the white velvet chaise-longue coverlet, and settled down by the fire with one of the guns and a can of oil. He looked meek and apologetic and offered to call a man he knew at the City Hall.

It took endurance to hunt Lillian. Chill and anxious, Mrs. Cugat wandered up one block and down another, through alleys and across strange gardens calling, 'Here, Lilli, Lilli — come, kitty!' in a persistent and weary falsetto. Curious faces peered at her from back windows and interested children vouchsafed conflicting information. However, as generally happened, just when she was ready to give up, she heard the familiar mew above her — far above her. Lillian was on a telephone pole this time — clinging galvanically with all four feet and looking fearfully down over her shoulder.

'Somebody's cat,' said a small boy conversationally at Mrs. Cugat's side, 'and he can't get down.'

'It's my cat,' said Mrs. Cugat hopelessly, peering up and shading her eyes with her hand.

'Don't he know what to do next?' inquired the tot interestedly.

'I guess not,' she said. 'Here, Lilli, Lilli — back up, you fool, and come down without looking!'

'If I was up there, I'd know what to do,' the boy said. Mrs. Cugat glanced at him. He looked as agile as a little spider.

'You couldn't climb up there and bring the kitty down, could you?' she ventured doubtfully. 'I'd give you a quarter if you would.'

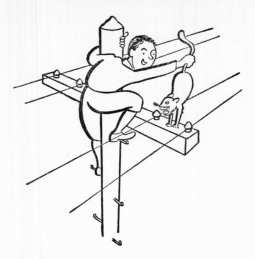

'Sure. Oh, boy! Give me a boost.'

Mrs. Cugat lifted him carefully up to the first rung and he started in sturdily to climb. The rungs were far apart, and she watched his small rubbers and blue-legginged legs with increasing anxiety. He was a littler boy than she'd realized.

'Are you all right?' she called foolishly when he was about three quarters of the way up.

'Sure,' he grunted without stopping. 'This is fun.'

Reassured, she bent her neck to ease it and then looked again. He had Lillian by the tail. 'Oh, be careful!' she called. 'Don't hurt her or she'll scratch you.'

A shriek tore the air. Mrs. Cugat swung around.

Reeling across the street came a blonde woman in lavender slacks. 'Hang on, Eddie!' she screamed. 'Mother's coming.' Eddie, up until this moment the personification of coolness and aplomb, let go Lillian's tail, peered over his own shoulder, and turned pale green. Then he let out a bellow. Doors popped open all along the street and people streamed out.

They called out the fire department in the end, and with it came the press. Eddie and Lillian aloft on their pole and again on the ground posed for the early editions. Mrs. Cugat gave her name and address — to everybody. Eddie's mother threatened suit. Eddie demanded his quarter. The crowd muttered menacingly. Mrs. Cugat, wondering what it felt like to be lynched, emptied her purse of three dollars and sixty cents. Then Eddie wanted to know if the lady'd let him keep the kitty. The crowd said, 'Aw — how cute!' and looked challenging. Clutching Lillian, Mrs. Cugat turned and fled up an alley.

When she reached home, however, she found the front door open and no one in sight but an unreliable-looking man cleaning his nails in the front hall.

'Did you want something?' she asked doubtfully, dumping Lillian, who threw up Mr. Cugat's chocolate cake and crawled off under a radiator.

'Harry Hirsch. I buy old clothes,' he explained briefly. 'The boss is getting me some.'

Anna and Belda and Mr. Cugat were in the store-room looking for that striped suit Mr. Cugat used to have. All the sealed moth bags had been unsealed, but they hadn't found it yet.

'I gave it to the Clothing Center, darling, two years ago. Hadn't you better get back to the library? There's no heat in here.'

Mr. Cugat had become diverted by his old navy uniform, which he hadn't seen in years. He was trying the coat on and throwing his shoulders back in front of the mirror. Moth balls rolled about on the floor. Anna and Belda were still with admiration. Harry Hirsch, presumably lonely, wandered in and joined them. When he got a good look at the storeroom, his eyes glistened, and he picked up one of Mr. Cugat's best winter overcoats and began going over it like a squirrel with a nut.

'A small size and plenty wore,' he said with relish. 'I'll give you a dollar and a half for it; there's no call for this kind of thing.'

Mr. Cugat, still in uniform, was coaxed back to the library and both a tan tablet and a pink tablet were administered — he couldn't remember which he'd had last. Harry Hirsch was coaxed to the front door by Mr. Cugat's winter overcoat and a checked golf suit thrown in at two dollars the lot. (No call, at all, for checks.) She had a feeling that now that he knew about the storeroom she would see more of him.

She cleaned up Lillian's chocolate cake and got back to the library, to find Mr. Cugat up on the bookcase ladder shifting things around on the top shelf and lighting the upper gloom with safety matches.

'What are you looking for?' she asked, regarding him thoughtfully.

'My Law School books. What's been done with them?'

Law School books? She didn't think she'd ever seen them. As a matter of fact, she didn't believe she even knew he'd ever been to Law School. Maybe they were at his mother's. They must be. Unconvinced, he remained disconsolately atop the ladder. She handed another tan pill up to him.

'God,' he mused, marveling and rummaging around again with renewed interest, 'doesn't anybody ever think to clean up here? It's positively filthy! Look——' A little cloud of dust rose to his righteous puff, but she wasn't looking. Her eyes were closed.

Then a bell pealed sharply. 'There's the doorbell,' he said, alert and clambering down. 'Is somebody going to answer it?'

'I don't know why not; they always have,' she said shortly, without opening her eyes.

'Oh — well — I was only wondering ——' Limp-
ing a little, he went over and took another tan pill,
let himself carefully down in his chair, and put his
head back with a sigh. 'Funny,' he said pensively,
'I'm weak as a kitten.'

Anna appeared in the door. 'Mr. Cartwright
and Mr. Sturm are here to see Mr. Cugat,' she announced. 'Mr. Cartwright's brought some things
from the office for Mr. Cugat to sign, if he's
able.'

'Mr. Cartwright! Good old Cory?' Mr. Cugat's
face lit up with the touching eagerness and incredulous gratitude of a man who has spent the past
ten years of his life on an island retreat of nuns.
'Tell 'em to come in here, Anna,' he said, removing
the chaise-longue coverlet with a walloping kick.
'And better bring some White Rock.' Mrs. Cugat
had opened her eyes again and was busily lighting
candles.

'Well, well! How's the invalid?' — 'Well, Georgie!
What's all this about?' — 'So they finally got you
down, did they?' In came the Messrs. Cartwright
and Sturm, looking fit, well combed, and ruddy.
Mrs. Cugat's heart smote her. Mr. Cugat in his
scarf and navy tunic and bathrobe, with his hair
sticking up, seemed frail and touching. *Was* frail
and touching.

'Do stay awhile and talk to him,' she urged,

hovering with little pats and a rush of renewed tenderness. 'It will do him good.'

Poor darling, she thought contritely, hurrying up the stairs for lipstick —— Were those pills strong enough? They gave one very little confidence, somehow. Perhaps she'd better have Doctor Buell drop in again tonight to check up. There was that weakness —— She left word for the doctor and then, suddenly weary, decided just to stay upstairs and take a bath.

Floating in pine oil and sipping a glass of hot milk, she grew relaxed and sentimental. Pathetic evidences of Mr. Cugat were all over the bathroom. His yesterday's shirt hung limply on a hook; his keys and wallet and watch huddled, abandoned, on the dressing-table; his shoes, with a look of discard, were unexpectedly under the washstand. Tears smarted behind her eyes as she looked at them.

There was a knock at the door. Anna's voice muted to a rasp came through. 'Mr. Cugat's asked the gentlemen to dinner!' She scrambled for her bathrobe and upset the milk. The voice deepened significantly. 'We're having them veal birds, you know.'

'What else, Anna?' she chattered, mopping at the milk.

'Squash.'

Veal birds and squash. Cory Cartwright was one

of those men who broil things over charcoal and make their own salad dressing. Howie Sturm's wife said her chef used to work at the Colony.

'Is Belda still here?' she hissed, sticking her head out.

'Just going.'

'Stop her and send her to the "A and P" for another steak and some lettuce and tomatoes and a quart of drugstore ice cream. You'll have to try Baked Alaska again, I'm afraid.'

Dinner was very late and the Baked Alaska much as usual — leaky. After four Old-Fashioneds, though, nothing matters. Nothing, anyway, but bed. Her throbbing head propped up by the chin and her eyes glazed, she listened through a meandering eternity to the wealth of detail embellishing what Cory Cartwright told the head waiter at the Ambassador about wild turkey — and about grouse (ruffed grouse) — and about woodcock — and about terrapin. 'Of *course* you were right, Cory!' she heard her own voice saying, far away. Mr. Cugat told Howie Sturm about that same old time at Reisenweber's with Connie Bennett; Anna, out beyond, banged dishes and rattled silver in a vicious tune.

But the doorbell finally rang. Anna, on her way to answer it, without her apron and apparently not caring who knew it, tossed an eloquent look. Was it the doctor at last? It was. Nothing goes on for-

ever; if one could only remember that. The Messrs. Sturm and Cartwright, taking a good deal of time over it, tactfully and jocosely withdrew. She waved them good-bye at the front door and sent her love to Mrs. Sturm. Then she went back to the library. Mr. Cugat, uninterrupted by the stethoscope, was telling Doctor Buell about Reisenweber's and Connie Bennett. Doctor Buell, also undeterred, produced a little silver funnel and peered into each of Mr. Cugat's ears.

'Well,' he said, folding everything up, 'you're a pretty good nurse, young lady!'

'I am?'

'Yes, I believe he'll be well enough to go back to

the office tomorrow. Now, if I might have just half a glass of water ——'

'Hell, doc,' said Mr. Cugat robustly, 'I don't need any more medicine!'

'No,' said Doctor Buell gently, 'but I think we'll just fix a little something for Mrs. Cugat.'

...*for richer, for poorer*...

WHEN Mrs. Cugat was fourteen this note appeared, penned despairingly, at the bottom of her report card:

'In Mathematics, Mary Elizabeth seems incapable of grasping anything beyond the simplest rudiments. The faculty, after serious consideration, are forced to recommend that she drop the subject entirely, as further attempts to master it appear useless.'

This ultimatum, deplorable as it seemed, was a tactful understatement. Mrs. Cugat had never come within a glimmer of grasping *any* mathematics — *even* the simplest rudiments. Otherwise a fairly alert child, she had sat through early arithmetic lessons blanketed with sickening incomprehension. Numbers, with their inscrutable laws and puzzling effects on each other, were seen by her as through a glass darkly, and she went on seeing them that way in spite of anything anybody could do. In time, being resourceful, she discovered that by simply memorizing a few rules of her own she could get along. Ten and something is always something-teen, but getting nine and anything is a lot of work because you have to do it with ten first and then subtract one from the answer; counting by fives is rhythmic and swinging like a poem, but counting by threes has to be done on the fingers; addition is forward and subtraction is back; if you want to divide by four just divide by two and then do it again; things like that.

She was still making do with these at the age of twenty, when, probably a victim of attracting opposites, she married Mr. Cugat, who sprang, mathematically mature, from a long line of bankers. Mr. Cugat was not exactly phenomenal, but manipulating figures and breathing air were much the same sort of thing to him — natural, effortless functioning. Some of the brightest hours of his childhood had been spent happily vacationing in a teller's cage. He added full-page columns of figures with graceful downward sweeps of the hand, and could probably have done your income tax for you while eating corn on the cob at the French Casino.

There were many things about Mrs. Cugat, the opposite to himself, which continued to charm him after the honeymoon and which he would not have had changed for the world. This passive inability

to cope with figures, however, was not one of them.
He began, almost at once, blithely confident, to do
something about it. There was no sense to it. It
simply showed lack of training and will-power.
Mrs. Cugat was a perfectly normal, rational being;
there was no reason at all why she should not keep
her checkbook in order, live within her budget, and
balance her household accounts. Mrs. Cugat knew
exactly what he meant. All her life people had been
saying this sort of thing. The only thing to do about
it, she had found, was just try to look intelligent,
do the best she could, and not get depressed. She
had held to these precepts in connection with
Mr. Cugat's tutelage since its beginning, and it
must be said in justice to both of them that Mr.
Cugat, while resigned to a long pull, still had
hope.

This morning, the eighteenth of the month — the
tenth, so strongly advocated by him, had a way of
slipping by her — she was sitting at her little Chinese
desk preparing to pay her bills. The desk was small
and upheld, in addition to a white leather desk set
of many pieces, a vase of chrysanthemums, a marble
clock, a bowl of peanuts, and a green china horse;
so that, with her checkbook, which was large and
businesslike, as became a banker's wife, there was
not much room left for the bills. They were heaped
in her lap and she was sorting them into three piles

on the floor — one to the right, one to the left, and
one behind her.

The three-pile system was an innovation of her
own — not recommended by Mr. Cugat — unknown,
in fact, to Mr. Cugat. To the right went the bills
which one paid with the smug promptness of the
substantial citizen — the Light and the Heat and
the Telephone, the Butcher, the Baker, the Candle-
stick Maker, and the Country Club. To the left
went other bills, those accompanied by reminders,
gentle or otherwise, and about which something
had better be done. To the back, sailing in a gay
arc over her head, went those which were *un*accompanied by reminders and which need worry
no one for a long time. The flaw in the system was
that there was very seldom enough left over after
the Right, Substantial Citizen Pile had been paid
to clean up the Left or Reminder Pile. She would
have to get down on the floor and spread the reminders out in rows for study, weighing the relative
importunity of each, and judiciously allotting her
last fifty dollars where it would do most to promote
her peace of mind.

This morning she finished sorting, had a peanut
or two, and then briskly, but with dread, attacked
the checkbook. This, as she had feared, was in bad
shape. Last month when she had written her checks
she had been miserable with a cold and simply not

up to carrying her balance along. Now, before anything else could be done, this would have to be attended to. It was very tiresome.

The clock ticked on, the peanut bowl diminished, and subsequently order was brought out of chaos. Order and exaltation! There is a first time for everything — all the Rights were paid, all the Lefts were paid, all the Back pile was stowed in the wastebasket, and she had *sixty-five dollars and twenty-seven cents* left over! What a heavenly feeling! She answered Anna's call to lunch with a bell-like lilt and skipped joyfully down the stairs, noting as she breezed along that the landing curtains were really very shabby. By the time she had reached her dessert — canned pears and Fig Newtons — she had acquired a high-salaried cook, new china, an oil painting for over the living-room mantel, slip covers for the porch, and a mink coat.

'You're wanted on the phone,' Anna said, breaking in on this spree brusquely.

It was The Chic Shop — and they had just got in some dear little knit suits which had brought Mrs. Cugat to mind the minute the box was opened. 'They look just like Mrs. Cugat,' everyone had exclaimed. Would she just drop in and *look* at them?

'How much are they?' Mrs. Cugat asked cannily. Knitted suits — she could use one, all right.

'Twenty-nine-fifty and up,' The Chic Shop re-plied reasonably, 'and all very unusual-looking.'

'Oh, yes. Well, I'm going out this afternoon, perhaps I'll have time to stop for a minute. Thank you for calling.' Hi-de-hi! Ho-de-ho! Twenty-nine-fifty! She'd better get two.

The Chic Shop housed itself in tasteful splendor. Smoky chromium mirrors, grape-colored carpets, and still white lamps. It was owned and presided over by one Max, who, besides being slim-hipped and broad-shouldered, had gray eyes, hair like sculptured tar, and only slightly Jewish features. When Mrs. Cugat arrived he was animatedly in-volved with a regal blonde dressed entirely in Persian lamb. Mrs. Cugat, welcomed by Miss Yvonne, slunk hurriedly into a fitting-room and resolved never to wear her polo coat in town again. This resolve was strengthened tenfold by Miss Yvonne's politely putting the polo coat on a hanger and hanging it, stained and drooping, under a very strong light.

'You'll love the little Knits,' she said enthusiasti-cally, helping Mrs. Cugat off with another rag. 'Jennifer is putting one on for you.'

'I'd rather try them on myself, I think. I can always tell better ——'

'You can? Oh. Most of *our* ladies prefer seeing things on the model. Just a minute, then.'

Jennifer successfully headed off, Mrs. Cugat was duly arrayed in a moss-green two-piece at seventy-five dollars and left to consider herself while Miss Yvonne went out to get a three-piece in rust. The twenty-nine-fifties, upon inquiry, proved to be sleeveless sweaters.

Max parted the gray velvet curtains. 'Hellew, there, Mrs. Cugat!' he said. 'Are you finding anything at all?' She revolved timidly before him. 'Take it off, my dear, it doesn't do a thing for you. Yvonne! Tell Axel to bring down that Schiaparelli with the silver-fox sleeves.'

The Schiaparelli with the silver-fox sleeves did do something for her; she could see it herself. So could everybody else. Miss Yvonne's chirrupy enthusiasm tensed up to reverent awe, and she was incapable of anything except an occasional breathless 'Lovely!' Max leaned against the door and said nothing at all, but he looked at Mrs. Cugat with the expression probably worn by the fairy godmother who fixed up Cinderella. Axel, who was small and grubby and foreign and a furrier, hung in the offing venting positive gutturals. The Persian lamb, urgently summoned, came and said 'Tebbly smot.' Hemmed in on all sides, Mrs. Cugat stood and regarded her mirrored image with sickening, hopeless fascination. The silver-fox sleeves sprang from her shoulders, thick and glistening; her hips, swathed

expertly in black 'imported weave,' looked very small; flowerlike and golden, her head rose proudly, framed in fur. She was another woman entirely.

'I hadn't thought of getting a coat,' she said once, rallying her strength. Several pairs of eyes glanced fleetingly at the polo coat, but nobody answered.

'On the tiny figure,' said Max finally, 'that's the perfect model, eh, Axel!' He turned back to Mrs. Cugat. 'I was almost afraid to buy it,' he said relievedly, with charming candor, 'but it was so outstanding, I just took the chance. They're darn few of my customers that could get away with it — I ran that risk. Yvonne, let's call Miss Lily, she'll want to see this.'

Miss Lily, mysteriously important, was on the

third floor taking a nap. Nevertheless, to see Mrs. Cugat in the Schiaparelli, everyone felt, would be worth her effort. She was reached by telephone and agreed.

While they waited, Mrs. Cugat diffidently broached the price. 'Two-twenty-five,' said Max. 'You can't touch the same thing at Hattie's for four hundred,' and brushed the matter aside. That seemed the end to that. Miss Lily arrived, looking frail and exhausted, and exclaimed, 'Ah, but yes!' To have waked her up and brought her all the way downstairs on a wild-goose chase would be nothing short of criminal.

Mrs. Cugat opened her mouth to say, 'Well, I suppose ——' and closed it to find that Axel had ripped off the collar with a razor blade and a little woman, appearing apparently out of the floor, was pinning up the hem. There was an air of general demobilization all around.

'You've got an important costume there,' said Max, halfway out the door, without giving it another look. 'I know you'll like it.' Miss Lily and the Persian lamb melted away. Axel departed without farewell. Miss Yvonne went to get her charge book. Mrs. Cugat, suddenly drained and exhausted, found herself alone, left to the drab ministering of the fitter. She revolved inch by inch on aching feet and they peered anxiously together into the mirror.

'It will look better when the pins are out, of course,' the fitter said encouragingly. Mrs. Cugat hoped so. The glamorous figure in the mirror had unaccountably vanished, leaving just Mrs. Cugat there, clothed in somewhat bunchy 'imported weave' with decidedly heavy silver-fox sleeves.

'Don't you want a couple of the little Knits to fill in?' asked Miss Yvonne brightly, popping back in with her book. But Mrs. Cugat thought not. All she wanted, quite suddenly, was to get the hell out.

She drove home absorbed, summoning justification. Of course, sooner or later, she would have had to buy a new coat anyway. This polo coat couldn't go on forever. And right now, when she had an extra sixty-five dollars, was certainly the time to do it. The sixty-five dollars being extra made the Schiaparelli with the silver-fox sleeves really only come to about a hundred and fifty dollars, and where again could she ever find that much silver fox for a hundred and fifty? Why, her mother's cape, which had only a few more skins, had cost seven hundred or so! Somewhat reassured and almost convinced of a bargain — another block farther would have done it — she turned up the driveway, and saw by the lights in the dressing-room windows that Mr. Cugat was already there.

A faintly sickening sense of guilt assailed her as

she climbed the stairs, but it was blown away by the breeziness of his greeting. 'Hi, darling,' he said, vigorously brushing his hair. 'I won the squash tournament!'

They had cocktails to celebrate. Dinner was pleasantly animated. Mr. Cugat gave a play-by-play account of his triumph, and she listened dutifully and lovingly and sipped her coffee, which, for once, was very good. Anna sang in the pantry, the radio struck up selections from *Show Boat*. Cloudless contentment enfolded her. The music swelled and rippled, and finishing his account, Mr. Cugat rose from the table and drew her into a close, slow fox trot. Mrs. Cugat loved to dance, particularly with Mr. Cugat, who, while slightly dated and on the whole unenthusiastic, was still very good. They circled slowly into the hall and he whistled tenderly a little off key. The cute thing, she thought, as he swooped on into the library. The music changed.

'Say, by the way,' he said briskly, suddenly through with dancing, 'I want to look at your books tonight. Charlie says you're overdrawn.'

Mrs. Cugat could feel life drain out of her. Numb weight took its place. 'He must be wrong. I couldn't be,' she said with no conviction.

'He's *never* wrong,' asseverated Mr. Cugat in a patient, familiar tone. 'Where are your books? I'll have to go over them and find out what you've

done.' He still sounded cheery and undismayed, but she sensed disaster as she led him upstairs.

He sat down squarely at her little desk and began systematically to remove its extraneous furnishings to the floor. 'All this junk,' he said, 'on a desk. No wonder you get balled up!' Mrs. Cugat handed him the checkbook and went over to sit by the dressing-table to await the cataclysm. 'Ole Man River, dat Ole Man River,' he hummed softly, coolly scrutinizing each stub and turning to the next. The clock ticked off several minutes and she got out a nail buffer to lessen the strain. 'He just keeps rollin', he keeps on rollin' —— ' She gave up buffing. 'What the ——,' he murmured, and she gave up breathing. 'Look here, what are all these checks written on the eighteenth? Why, that's today!'

'I know, I didn't get around to the bills until today,' she admitted apologetically.

'Good God! Have you mailed the checks out yet?

'Certainly,' she replied virtuously.

Mr. Cugat turned slowly to look at her; he looked unblinkingly for a full minute, defeat in his eyes. 'It was this morning,' he said finally, 'that your account showed the overdraft; since then you've written and mailed out about three hundred dollars in checks —!' Mrs. Cugat looked horrified but uncomprehending. 'I don't see how you do it,' he concluded, wonder in his tone.

He found out, though, after a time. It was mostly that old business of having to borrow when subtracting. Mrs. Cugat found it hard to remember when she'd borrowed and when she hadn't. Especially when she had to skip over one or two zeros and change them all into nines. (There was a foolish and complicated rule if ever there was one!) 'Well, darling,' he said, going back for one more grim look and closing the book with a bang, 'that's the worst you've ever done. You've got three hundred and eleven dollars in checks coming through and nothing to meet them but a twenty-one-dollar overdraft! God alone knows why, but you seem to have added several of the larger amounts last month in-

stead of subtracting them; and your book,' he concluded in final reproach, 'is full of peanut shells.'
Whereupon he rose, disrobed, and went to bed without taking further notice of her.

Her night, not unnaturally, was miserable. As
far as the checkbook and overdraft and the outstanding checks were concerned, she comforted
herself, as she had done before, by telling herself
that, after all, she had done the best she could —
no one could do more. Although, as the night wore
on and the débâcle appeared each hour more spectacular, pictures of Mr. Cugat pawning the family
pearls, falsifying his accounts to cover her, getting
dramatically arrested and perhaps shooting himself
kept reappearing and had to be thrust sensibly aside.
The thing that worried her to the point of suffocation
was Max's Schiaparelli with the silver-fox sleeves!
Would morning ever come so she could call him up
and tell him that she had changed her mind? It
wasn't exactly what she wanted. She would come
in again and choose something else. What time was
it now? Only three-thirty. Why did life have to
be like this? Why did *she* have to be like this —
weak-minded, stupid, and rightly unloved?

Morning finally did come, of course, and Mr.
Cugat seemed much the same as on any other morning. He never said much in the morning anyway,
so she couldn't tell what the state of his mind might

be. He read his paper and ate his egg and departed with his usual abstracted kiss, leaving no clue.

Max, the sybarite, finally reached at his place of business at eleven-thirty, was agreeableness itself. 'Ew, Mrs. Cugat,' he said comfortingly, 'don't have a moment's doubt. I wouldn't let you have it if it weren't the perfect thing on you.' Mrs. Cugat said she realized that. It was a lovely coat, but, on thinking it over, it was really more than she'd thought of paying, so if —— He grew a little stern. 'I'm afraid it's too late to get it out of the workroom now,' he said. 'Axel's been on it all morning. However' — his voice became kind again — 'don't think about the price, my dear. I don't want to see it on anybody but you! Pay me later — I'll tell you, I'll not bill you with it until next month and you can just forget it till then.'

This seemed very nice of Max and appeared to settle the matter. She hung up the receiver and went to look disconsolately out of the window. Today was the Garden Club luncheon, but she had no heart for people or gardens, much less a stomach for food. She'd take Lillian and go out along the lake shore — maybe stay all day. She went dispiritedly up the stairs and was almost ready — heavy shoes, sandwich, and small sad book of poems, with Lillian ensconced and purring in her basket, when the phone rang.

'Mr. Cugat calling Mrs. Cugat,' the telephone girl at the bank said crisply.

Mr. Cugat took several minutes; she could hear him busily talking on another line and sounding brusque and authoritative. Her hand grew moist on the receiver. Then, 'Hello, honey,' he said cheerily. 'Henry was just in and wants us to eat at the club tonight — he has somebody here from out of town. We aren't doing anything, are we?'

'No, I guess not,' she replied meekly.

'OK. Meet us there around seven, we're going to play squash. Oh, yes, I deposited four hundred dollars in your account this morning. Go, right now, and enter it in your checkbook, *subtract* your overdraft and don't write any more checks again without calling me first. Good-bye, sweet; see you tonight.'

Well! Warm, sweet relief welled up and flooded through her. Everything was all right again. Her world slid back into focus and took on color. Was there anybody in the world quite as wonderful as Mr. Cugat! How could he be so patient and forgiving with such an idiotic little fool as she? She went to her desk and carefully did as he said. Darling Mr. Cugat! Fixing her account up again just as if there had never been anything wrong with it. Fixing it up even better — now she had sixty-seven dollars extra! My, she was hungry! She would go to the Garden Club after all. The sun came out and birds sang in the yard; she got out her new print and white gloves.

While she was dressing, Anna brought in the mail. It was small and uninteresting except for one heavy, crested envelope that looked like a royal summons, but proved to be, when opened, an announcement from a New York haberdasher heralding a sale of men's silk dressing-gowns reduced to sixty-five dollars (monogram extra). There was a sketch of an Apollo wearing one and a small accompanying swatch of plum-colored brocade. The sketch pleased her, and she reflected that Mr. Cugat would look nice in a plum-colored dressing-gown. That brown woollen thing he clung to was anything but flatter- ing. How she would love to give him a new dress-

ing-gown as a surprise! Darling Mr. Cugat, so patient and forgiving — sixty-five dollars, while rather a lot for a dressing-gown, was nothing to the gratitude and love she felt toward him. Sixty-five dollars. Her account was all fixed up again — *and there was sixty-seven extra dollars in it!* How simply grand! She could get the dressing-gown! To spend her extra money on him instead of on herself seemed a very nice gesture; it sort of evened things up, since he had been so kind about her mistakes.

Warm with generosity, she impulsively took off her gloves and sat down and wrote the letter. One plum brocade dressing-gown, size medium, mono-grammed G. E. C. in gray-blue. Special price sixty-five dollars. Send and charge.

It wasn't until she had mailed it, on the way to the Garden Club, that she remembered Max. Panic froze her, and she stood in wide-eyed horror as the mailbox banged shut. Then she dropped her hands and, taking a deep breath, started shakily on her way. Oh, well, she thought, pulling herself together resolutely, his bill isn't coming until next month. *Anything* might happen before next month.

. . . and to obey? . . .

'THE CORYELLS have a very fancy guest visiting them,' Mrs. Cugat announced one night from the edge of the bathtub, where she was perched, watching Mr. Cugat, just home from the office, wash up before dinner.

Mr. Cugat snapped a wet finger in her direction. 'What's that to us?' he inquired airily.

'I asked some people here to meet him Thursday night.'

'Oh.' Then he ventured, 'I thought you and Brigit Coryell didn't like each other ——'

'We don't,' Mrs. Cugat said, and went on reasonably, 'That's why I'm having them — I just want to show her and her old celebrity what a nice party I can have.'

'Oh,' said Mr. Cugat again. 'I see.' But he didn't.

'She's all agog because his picture was in *Town*

and Country — she let it drop about four times,' Mrs. Cugat went on disdainfully.

'What's he celebrated for?' he asked.

'He's got the highest batting average, or something, of any cricket-player in the United States.'

Mr. Cugat peered over his towel. '*Cricket*-player?'

'Yes, he plays cricket. It's good to bat a lot of times in cricket,' she explained, 'and this man's batted *more* times than any other man on the Long Island Old Boys team!'

'Well!' Mr. Cugat chortled. '*Fancy!*'

'Well —' Mrs. Cugat protested defensively, 'he's *very* good, if you want to know.'

'I'll bet,' said Mr. Cugat. 'Can he keep that funny score and everything?'

She turned her back, so then he said, 'Who'd you ask to meet this lad?'

'The Blakes and the Taylors — I thought they'd go well.'

He grimaced. 'Ah — café society.' Then he sighed, 'Aren't you going to have Cory?'

'No; he's too liable to get funny. This party's going to be really smart. I'll show Brigit Coryell — née Mahoney — a thing or two.'

'Well,' said Mr. Cugat resignedly, 'let's just try and forget it until Thursday.'

Mrs. Cugat, needless to say, did not forget it until Thursday — nor try. She went to work on it that very night, telephoning to the caterer and making lists of things (including a copy of *Town and Country*) to be borrowed from her mother. It was to be a dinner perfectly planned and executed — one of deceiving casualness and simplicity, but without a flaw.

Mr. Cugat, peering over her shoulder late in the evening at the myriad lists under her pen, said, 'What do the Old Boys do — travel on their stomachs?'

Mrs. Cugat waved him away, 'It's not that cricket-player I'm taking all these pains for,' she explained simply. 'It's for Brigit and Lois — you wouldn't understand.'

Mr. Cugat looked as if, indeed, he would not, and draped himself over the back of her chair.

'Pheasants in Cream yet!' he exclaimed, and read on with relish: 'Purée of Watercress! Romaine, Orange, and Almond Salad! Iced Zabaione!' Then he said, suddenly wistful, that he didn't suppose *anything* could be done about Anna *always* boiling his three-minute eggs for ten minutes *every* morning, could there?

'Not this week,' said Mrs. Cugat briefly.

Thursday dawned and all was in readiness: silver shone and mirrors gleamed. By noon the dining-room was ready and Mrs. Cugat complacently viewed it from the door. No flowers, ferns, or salted nuts, with their partified effects, were to be seen; the table, bare save for some brunette lace, was simply graced by a silver épergne of peaches and four soaring dark-green candles. The air was still and icy because she planned to use the grate. Firelight and candlelight — so effective and, she always thought, somehow Continental. The room, unfortunately, heated like a kiln, so pre-refrigeration was essential. Pleasant, unfamiliar odors drifted from the kitchen, and the sound of something being chopped in a wooden bowl spattered the shining silence. Everything she could think of was done — not a detail overlooked — and then, in the back hall, the telephone rang.

'It's him,' a perspiring Anna announced briefly from the pantry door. Oh, yes, she thought —

about the wine — and sped to the extension in the library.

'Bunker of the Consolidated is here,' said Mr. Cugat's voice in the clipped, formal accents which proclaimed that he was not alone. 'I'm bringing him out to dinner.'

Mrs. Cugat gave a little sort of mew. 'George,' she breathed, 'you can't!'

Mr. Cugat cleared his throat heavily. 'OK?' he queried in a bright false tone. 'Fine! we'll be along about seven.'

'Darling,' she hissed, 'we're having that dinner party tonight — you know, for the Coryells' guest ——'

'Oh — ah — yes. Fine, uh — fine, *fine!* More the merrier, what!'

'Tonight of all nights!' she wailed.

Mr. Cugat became jocose. 'Be sure there's plenty to eat,' he warned playfully. 'Bunker here' (here Bunker was palpably prodded) 'looks like he knew good food!'

'God,' said Mrs. Cugat, 'with six vice-presidents, why am I always chosen to feed the customers?'

'Four vice-presidents,' said Mr. Cugat automatically. 'Well, see you later!'

Bunker of the Consolidated! She'd have to set the table all over again! She went to gaze mournfully at its still perfection. 'I won't do it!' she said with sudden spirit, and stalked back to the library.

'I won't do it!' she said bravely to Mr. Cugat when she got him on the phone. Mr. Cugat was silent for a full minute, then he said briefly in an unfamiliar voice, 'Yes, Liz.'

'I must?'

'Yes.'

She put down the phone slowly. Well, that was that. One more man couldn't make much difference, though, she comforted herself, and the Consolidated sounded like a New York bank. It might be worse. Of course she would have to put a leaf in the table, and that meant that the space between the right-hand corner and the sideboard would be just barely wide enough to let Anna, who was broad of beam, through. It *did* let her through — but Mrs. Cugat had found that Anna breathed heavily with anxiety while negotiating it, which did not contribute to the unobtrusiveness of the service. On the other hand, if the sideboard was moved along a little, a dust mark showed on the wall; but, of course, by candlelight this might not be noticed. It seemed the lesser of the two evils. Sighing, she went to look for the extra table leaf.

Seven o'clock found the Blakes, Taylors, Coryells, and the pride of the Old Boys assembling. There had been no further word of Mr. Cugat and Bunker. The Blakes, Taylors, and Coryells were all looking

uncommonly sleek and languid and talking like
people in a play — due presumably to the O. B.,
whose name was Mr. Pidgeon. Mr. Pidgeon appeared to be up among the clouds, but he descended
politely to be introduced and said Mrs. Cugat
looked familiar, was it Nassau? Mrs. Cugat said no,
she'd never been to Nassau. Cannes, then? No.
Sun Valley? No. The Grand National *last* year?
She was afraid not. Mr. Pidgeon subsided.

'St. Moritz?' suggested Mrs. Cugat, who had
never been there either, but was determined to go
down fighting.

'Possibly,' said Mr. Pidgeon, but looked very
doubtful — so did everybody else.

'George,' she explained apologetically, 'isn't home
from downtown yet. I hope he hasn't been kept
at the bank.'

'George,' said Mrs. Coryell, in rueful explanation
to Mr. Pidgeon, 'has only one interest in life —
business.' Mr. Pidgeon looked suitably appalled;
so did Mrs. Blake, whose husband's one interest in
life was whiskey, and Mrs. Taylor, whose husband's
one interest in life was gin. Mr. Blake and Mr.
Taylor looked blank, a customary expression.

'Do you know Chubby Wescott?' Mr. Pidgeon
inquired.

'*Wes*cott?' Mrs. Cugat said. No, she didn't believe she did.

Mr. Pidgeon looked disappointed. '*He's* taken a job,' he said.

Mrs. Coryell then took a cocktail and idled across the room to peer with narrowed eyes at a group of etchings on the far wall. 'I love this house,' she said, 'it's so simple.' Then she looked closer at the etchings and shook her head — just a little — to herself. 'I see that Dégas that Duveen had here a few years ago was sold again,' she said in a bell-like voice to the world at large. 'I couldn't bear it myself and I told him so. I said, "Joe, I wouldn't own it!" You can imagine — he was floored.'

Mrs. Taylor said to Mr. Blake, 'Naturally Florida and California are both a bore, but where else is there!'

Mr. Coryell said to Mrs. Blake, 'As luck would have it I was paired with Hagen ——'

'Cartier's didn't have a thing I wanted,' Mrs. Blake replied.

'Cripps-Fuller's actions are anything but upright,' Mr. Pidgeon said to somebody, 'but I will say this for him, he conceals his googlies.' Some uncertainty greeted this, so he added by way of explanation, 'He's a right-handed leg break,' and turned to Mrs. Cugat. 'Do you know Dogo and Muffin Cripps-Fuller?' he asked hopefully. No, Mrs. Cugat didn't think so. Disappointment claimed him again.

'What can have happened to George?' she worried. 'He didn't say he'd be late. I suppose he's had to wait to bring that man.'

'What man, darling?' Everybody stopped saying things. 'Don't tell me some kindred captain of industry?'

'Some New York banker,' said Mrs. Cugat shortly.

'One of the Morgans?' squealed Mrs. Taylor.

'His name's Bunker, I believe,' Mrs. Cugat said, and all looked as if they'd thought as much except Mr. Pidgeon, who asked, 'Old Wately Bunker, the squash racquets man?' To Mrs. Cugat this seemed unlikely, but she prayed to God it was.

'It might be,' she said. 'He's very prominent,' and checked herself warily.

'I wonder if we know him,' said Mrs. Blake anxiously. A key turned in the front door.

'Here they are!' Mrs. Cugat exclaimed relievedly, and sped to the hall. When she got there, Mr. Cugat was putting his key back into his pocket, on his face an expression she had never seen before; he looked frightened. Behind him crowded three people, two women with blonde hair and a man with none.

'Mrs. Bunker — Mrs. Cugat — Mrs. Cugat — Mr. Bunker,' mumbled Mr. Cugat, without meeting her eye.

'And Sister,' beamed one of the blondes, shoving the other one forward.

'Pleased-to-meet-you-I'm-sure,' said Sister.

'How do you do?' said Mrs. Cugat; 'the maid will take your things,' and smiled without even knowing it. Sister and the Bunkers trooped upstairs.

'Don't look at me like that, Liz,' Mr. Cugat implored in a hoarse whisper. 'He didn't have them along this morning. They're motoring through and only just turned up. I've been sweating all the way home — I was almost scared to come in.'

She looked at him and saw that actually he looked shattered. It gave her strength. 'We'll manage somehow,' she said, a little dazedly, trying not to glare, and sped to the kitchen.

Back in the living-room, after a doughty fifteen minutes, her eyes hunted Bunker of the Consolidated and found him perched on the piano bench, holding a highball and looking meek. Trying hard, Providence could have produced no one looking less like the very prominent New York banker of her hopes — quite definitely he was not old Wately, the squash racquets man. He was little and roly-poly, had bright red eyebrows, a gold stickpin, and high shoes. Disappointment in him was, however, a bagatelle compared to the dismay which burgeoned in her bosom upon her second look at Mrs. Bunker and Sister.

Mrs. Bunker and Sister were not looking at all meek. They were looking bright-eyed and arch, and the aroused interest of the Messrs. Coryell, Blake, and Taylor was noticeable. Mrs. Bunker's and Sister's cheeks were doll-pink, their hair doll-curly, and they had lovely curves; also, you could see, they had on new dresses and they felt like a party. The air had changed. Mr. Cugat, briskly helping his mother-in-law's butler supply the demand, looked better. The heavens had not fallen upon his awful arrival and relief was sweet; he had the utmost faith in Mrs. Cugat's domestic maneuverings — she had never failed him yet; she had been to the kitchen and now was back — Bunker of the Consolidated would be fed. Mr. Pidgeon, shunted to a corner, was inquiring if anybody knew a right-handed off-break bowler named Jergens-Axel-Jergens, and the Mesdames Coryell, Blake, and Taylor, in the corner with him, were saying that they thought they did. Mrs. Cugat braced herself to steer a nightmare.

But she figured without Sister. Sister with a few Martinis in her was a natural-born party-steerer. She was a riot. Always had been, Mrs. Bunker explained in an aside to Mrs. Cugat. In fact, she confided, sometimes people hardly knew what to make of Sister. Mr. Bunker's people, among others.

Dinner went off like a breeze — or perhaps more like a gale. Hardly what Mrs. Cugat had so lovingly planned. There was no firelight, for one thing —

Mr. Cugat, backed between the andirons, would have been barbecued. Mrs. Cugat and, by some dreadful mischance, Mr. Pidgeon occupied low library chairs under the eaves of the sideboard with their eyes at plate-level and Anna squeezed stentoriously in and out between them, perspiring freely. The kitchen door, because of its free swing, spanked Mrs. Coryell on the rebound of every exit, and finally had to be propped open, to reveal bedlam beyond. However, thanks to the caterer, who always planned on some to take home, the food went around and, thanks to the Consolidated, an apparently valued connection, the champagne flowed. Sister, a riot on Martinis, with champagne developed into a first-class furor and did a parody on 'My Heart Belongs to Daddy'; Mrs. Bunker revealed an unexpected and lively talent for rhymed toasts. Bunker said very little, but after the fifth toast ('Bottoms *up*, everybody!'), he smiled shyly at Mrs. Cugat over the rim of his glass. He had a cute face, Mrs. Cugat decided from the rim of her fifth bottom up — a little like Dopey the Dwarf. His gold stickpin fascinated her — it looked like an inlay. It wasn't, Mr. Bunker said, twinkling with pleasure at being asked; it was just the first gold nugget he had ever found. Mr. Pidgeon, swept before the storm, looked baffled — nobody seemed to know *any*body he did.

After dinner Mrs. Cugat, by admirable management and a firm hand, got three tables of bridge under way, but a fractious disinclination to stay put was soon evident. The Messrs. Taylor and Blake, with Sister and Mrs. Bunker, mutinied almost at once and repaired to the sun-porch to dance, and one by one, as each man found himself dummy, the ranks thinned.

'Where's Mr. Pidgeon?' Mrs. Cugat inquired anxiously of Mrs. Coryell, who came to fill in at the one table left.

'Out in the pantry with the rest of them,' Mrs. Coryell said dryly.

'What on earth are they doing out there?'

'Well, darling, they've got a hat on the floor and they're trying to pitch playing cards into it at ten cents a card — Mr. Bunker's game.' From the sun-porch, the strains of the victrola, overlaid by Mrs. Bunker's rich laugh, floated gaily.

'One spade,' said Mrs. Blake icily.

'Pass,' said Mrs. Coryell. 'Don't you love people who call stockings hose?'

'Three hearts,' said Mrs. Taylor, with a baleful look at the door.

'Pass,' said Mrs. Cugat, not looking at her hand. One more hour and she'd have to send out for more Scotch.

'Mrs. Bunker and Sister thought your peach centerpiece was novel,' remarked Mrs. Coryell; 'and as for your *drapes!*'

'Easy there, big boy!' Sister's voice rang out clearly. 'What's the matter, haven't you any home-life?' Bridge was abandoned in a concerted movement.

'Rescue Mr. Pidgeon, will you, Liz?' Mrs. Coryell shrugged amusedly. 'We'll really have to push along.' Mrs. Cugat sped to the pantry.

Mr. Pidgeon and Mr. Bunker were still there — Mr. Pidgeon looking soured and the corners of his mouth tight. 'Never mind, Cricket,' Mr. Bunker was saying kindly. 'You'll get it — it will come all of a sudden. Just hold the card between your first two fingers, relax, and flip. You understand?'

'Quite,' said Mr. Pidgeon grimly.

'Well,' said Mr. Cugat, stretching pleasurably as the door finally closed on the last of the Bunkers, 'that was a pretty good party, after all.' Mrs. Cugat glared wordlessly. 'What's the matter, honey?' he protested. 'People had fun, didn't they?'

'Yes — people have fun at Coney Island, too,' said Mrs. Cugat in a light, tight voice. Then she went on tremulously: 'My lovely party — that I planned so carefully! It's nothing to you, I suppose, that all my trouble was wasted and I've been made a perfect laughing-stock!'

'Aw, honey,' said Mr. Cugat.

Mrs. Cugat drew away. 'If I'd had any backbone

at all, I'd have just refused to have him in the first place and everything would have been all right. Next time I'll know better. Who do you think you are, anyway — giving out orders like a Sultan! It's the last time you'll get away with it around here, I can tell you!' Mr. Cugat looked penitent, but she was not through. 'Fun! I suppose you think Mr. Pidgeon had fun. He must think we're barbarians — he looked simply disgusted!'

'He dropped eight dollars and a half in that hat game,' said Mr. Cugat, with a glint of pleasure, 'and it damned near killed him. That wasn't disgusted he was looking; that was broken-hearted.'

'George!' she said horrified, 'how dreadful! You fix it right up tomorrow at the Coryells' tea.'

'The Coryells' *tea?*' said Mr. Cugat. 'I'm not going to any tea.'

'Oh, yes, you are,' she said, with a sudden glint in her own eye; 'and you're wearing a cutaway.'

Mr. Cugat laughed. 'Fat chance,' he said lightly. 'Remember me? I work for a living.'

'You're going to the Coryells' tea,' said Mrs. Cugat, 'if it closes the bank. But I imagine,' she added cuttingly, 'they'll manage to stay open.'

Mr. Cugat looked suddenly meek. 'I *must?*' he queried.

'Yes.'

The Coryells lived in a Normandy farmhouse

that was usually mistaken for a country club. 'Brigit must have asked *every*body!' Mrs. Cugat murmured, viewing the ranks of parked cars in the cobbled courtyard at five the next afternoon. Then she added testily, 'We're late, of course.'

Mr. Cugat, beautiful in ascot and shining hat, silently took his car check from the attendant and looked bleak. 'Everybody's here, all right,' the attendant vouchsafed chattily, 'even the Governor.' At this Mr. Cugat looked somewhat comforted, but once within the portals, pushing through the strident throng, bleakness returned — there weren't very many men. Everybody's wife, however, in her gayest plumage, had rallied to *Town and Country's* call. They knotted around the silver punchbowls, clustered over the groaning board, and clogged the stairway. Little maids in lavender moiré squeezed in and out bearing plates of molded salad, decorated ice cream, and assorted patty shells. Mr. Cugat, plowing dutifully along in Mrs. Cugat's wake, had one thrust upon him and accepted it mutely, but he averted his eyes. Through the crowd at the end of the room, Mrs. Coryell could be glimpsed beaming over an inordinate corsage — at her side, the Governor. Mr. and Mrs. Cugat, after edging patiently along, made a final plunge and broke into the clear; as the ranks parted, Mrs. Cugat blinked. Between the Governor and a radiant Mrs. Coryell stood a

chubby figure with bright-red eyebrows and a gold stickpin. The gubernatorial voice was rolling in sonorous introduction.

'My very distinguished visitor, Mr. Horace P. Bunker,' it boomed, 'of whom you have no doubt heard!' Then His Excellency bent confidentially and rumbled behind his hand, 'Our next ambassador to Saint James's, you know.'

Mrs. Coryell's smile all but split her face. Mr. Bunker bobbed his head and then caught sight of Mrs. Cugat. 'Hi,' he whispered.

The Governor turned. 'Hello, Cugat, my boy. Nice to see you! Bunker, here, tells me you gave him a beautiful dinner last night!'

'Thank you, sir,' said Mr. Cugat. 'My wife gets

credit for that.' Mrs. Cugat, blushing prettily, squeezed his arm in precipitate apology.

'It was *marvelous*,' Mrs. Coryell said fervently.

'Where's Mr. Pidgeon, Bridge?' Mr. Cugat asked politely.

Mrs. Coryell looked momentarily blank; then she bethought herself. 'Oh, Mr. *Pidgeon*,' she said carelessly. 'Up in his room, I believe, throwing cards in his hat.'

... *let no man put asunder* ...

MR. J. DUNCAN ATTERBURY, president of the Tri-State Trust, emerged through wide screen doors onto his shady veranda and, contentedly patting his well-tailored paunch, went to sit in a deep wicker rocker. He was followed by his wife, who briskly wielded a palmleaf fan and was herself followed by the Cugats; Mr. Cugat contentedly patting what would, inevitably, be a paunch by the time he was president of the Tri-State Trust, Mrs. Cugat wishing she had a fan. These three disposed themselves, likewise, upon chintz and wicker.

'It's very hot,' said Mr. Atterbury, serenely viewing his broad lawns through a scud of mellow smoke.

'Yes, sir,' said Mr. Cugat, and flicked the ash inexpertly from another of Mr. Atterbury's cigars.

Mrs. Cugat, too heavy with food to embroider this, put her head back lazily and wondered, behind half-closed lids, why cigars should give an air of substance to men over fifty and make all men under forty look like horse-traders. Mrs. Atterbury, humming lightly, rose, plucked two dried geranium heads from a window box, killed a fly, emptied an ash tray, and went to sit in the swing.

'Mary Elizabeth looks all washed out, George,' she said pleasantly.

Mr. Cugat and Mr. Atterbury removed their cigars to look at Mrs. Cugat in concern. Hastily recalling animation, Mrs. Cugat protested vivaciously that she had never felt better in her life, and then stirred with resentment. Anybody'd look all washed out who had been obliged to sit through church and a four-course noon dinner with the thermometer at nearly a hundred — particularly after almost no sleep! Often had she and Mr. Cugat marveled together that the Atterburys' occasional Sunday dinners should so invariably and relentlessly follow on the heels of a late party. Dinners which, of course, were not to be protested.

'It's all this heat,' Mrs. Atterbury went on ruefully. 'You children aren't staying home, I hope.'

'I took my vacation in the spring,' Mr. Cugat hastened to explain; 'don't you remember? We had a whole month in Bermuda — two weeks more than I rated,' he added with a grateful look to his employer.

'Spring,' chided Mrs. Atterbury, impelling her energetic palm breeze in Mrs. Cugat's direction, 'was months ago! Surely you don't intend to keep a fragile little thing like Mary Elizabeth here *all summer!*' Mrs. Cugat, who, though undersized, was as tough as a turtle, looked pleased. 'Why didn't your mother take you on that cruise with her?' Mrs. Atterbury inquired of her indignantly.

Mrs. Cugat hastened to her parent's defense. 'Oh, she asked me,' she exclaimed, 'but I wouldn't leave George all alone.'

'Fuff!' said Mrs. Atterbury to that, 'it would do him good. I'll tell you what you're going to do — you're going up to Winnisocket with me next week for at least a month. If George doesn't know enough to look after you, someone else will have to. You don't look *at all strong* to me!' Mr. Cugat, distressed, regarded his wife in unfamiliar anxiety.

'Splendid idea!' beamed Mr. Atterbury, who liked having his kindly and artless hand in another's destiny. 'Mary Elizabeth does look frail.'

Mrs. Cugat, who by this time could feel herself slipping away like Beth in *Little Women*, rallied frantic strength to protest. No! No! she couldn't think of it! Really. It was out of the question. She would love it, of course — she had always longed to see Winnisocket — it was sweet of them to want her — but, just now, no. She couldn't

possibly leave George. She was perfectly all right —
just something she ate and a restless night.

But she didn't have a chance; by five o'clock and
time to go home, definite plans were emerging and,
wholly spent, she was surreptitiously taking her own
pulse.

'Do you feel up to getting supper?' Mr. Cugat
asked tenderly when they reached the house —
empty of Anna and Sunday-quiet.

'Certainly I feel up to it,' she replied with asperity.
'There is nothing the matter with me and you
know it. I just had no sleep and a hangover and all
that dinner. You don't look any too well yourself!'

'You seem pale and limp,' Mr. Cugat persisted.

'I'm always pale in hot weather,' Mrs. Cugat said, exasperated, 'and I look limp because of my hair; I need a new permanent, but I'm waiting for the back to grow. I think it was very rude of everybody to sit there all afternoon and say how awful I looked. The way you talked, anybody'd think you *wanted* me to leave you! I could have gone to Jamaica, you know; I guess maybe I should have — nobody seems to need me around here!' Whereupon she flung herself down on the couch and burst into tears.

'There, there, honey,' protested Mr. Cugat, alarmed. 'You see, there *is* something wrong with you,' and he knelt with encircling arms, for which he received a smart clout on the ear. Mrs. Cugat wept afresh and with relish.

But the storm, furious as a summer cloudburst, abated as immediately. 'You're *sure* you don't want me to go?' she snuffed, snuggling suddenly back into his warily returning embrace.

'Darling, no, no,' he vowed in a lulling voice, but a somewhat contemplative look in his eye, 'of course not!'

'And you'll tell the Atterburys the first thing in the morning?'

'First thing.'

'All right, then, that's that,' she said, and sat up refreshed.

'Lie there,' he said firmly. 'I'll go get out the

sandwiches and make a mint julep or something; this has been a hell of a day — you're worn out.'

Mrs. Cugat sank back submissively and closed her eyes. Maybe she *wasn't* very strong. Was she destined to be just a memory? — a faded photograph — sweet-faced — outmoded — George's first wife, who had died so young? She ought to have some new pictures taken. Out in the kitchen, Mr. Cugat dropped a plate or something and cursed quietly; her lips curved in a soft smile — some day he might look back and be glad he had been able to do her these few little services ——

This other-world gentleness was dispelled almost immediately by the mint julep. A creeping zest for life took its place. A trip to Winnisocket was not to be sneezed at. Would Mr. Cugat actually benefit, as Mrs. Atterbury said? Ought she to go, perhaps for *his* sake? It had been a long time since he had tasted bachelorhood and, although he dieted cheerfully enough on matrimony, one heard that occasional respite was good for husbands. For her part, she'd almost forgotten what it felt like to be free and on her own. Winnisocket would be another world — new faces, new experiences, broadening influences — even, perhaps, adventure. If she was ever going to encounter broadening influences or adventure, she'd better hurry up — pretty soon she'd be thirty. She finished her mint julep and pleasantly fashioned

herself a small adventure at Winnisocket: the hero,
looking like Anthony Eden: she, in all new clothes.
She'd need a lot of new clothes ——

The Winnisocket House nestled amid fashionable
old mountains and looked like a mad pastrycook's
dream. It was turreted and crenelated and iced
with pistache stucco and it had a thousand rooms.
It also had two swimming pools, two golf courses,
two orchestras, a landing field, and courts for everything. Mrs. Cugat, spinning along in the Atterburys' station wagon, caught her first glimpse of it
across a valley and thrilled. Suffering from a bad
case of cold feet, it was her first thrill since leaving
home. Her trunk was full of lovely new clothes and
her purse was full of American Express checks, and
the domestic arrangements of Mr. Cugat and Anna
gave every promise of running on oiled wheels —
both had repeatedly begged her not to give them
a thought, both had assured her cheerfully that
they would get along somehow — but she had been
depressed.

They were just too damned cheerful; she had a
suspicion that they were both almost looking forward to 'getting along somehow.' Happily 'getting
along somehow' was Anna's natural habitude; it
took a good deal of chivvying to keep her to the
mark — and Mrs. Cugat had serious doubts as to

whether Mr. Cugat would chivvy Anna at all.
Even before she left they had had the chummy air
of confederates. 'When you and I are running
things, Anna,' Mr. Cugat had remarked, 'we won't
have *any* desserts, will we?' Anna had chuckled in-
dulgently and then hummed in the pantry. Mr.
Cugat, of course, had reiterated ardently that he
would miss her, but, just the same, there had been
a light in his eye. She had boarded the train spirit-
lessly and gone straight to bed.

The Winnisocket House, however, spires twinkling
and flags flying in the morning sun, rekindled anti-
cipation; Mr. Cugat and Anna receded.

The car passed a long string of saddled horses;
a gray roadster swept by, driven by a deeply tanned
girl in a yellow sweater; a man in shorts on a bicycle
waved gaily; the Olde Maides' Tea Shoppe announced a sale of maple sugar; the Olde Shedde
Players announced *Victoria Regina*; arrows pointed
the way to 'The Caves.' By the time the station
wagon had rolled under the Winnisocket House's
vaulting porte-cochère, she was, after all, glad she'd
come. Mrs. Atterbury, who had preceded her by
a few days, appeared with two friends and a battery
of bellboys and greeted her affectionately; one of
the friends asked if she didn't think the air was like
wine — which indeed it was — and the other said,
'Fred will be so *glad* you've arrived!' Mr. Cugat and
Anna vanished and she got out her lipstick.

Five days later found her at breakfast reading Mr. Cugat's one letter for perhaps the tenth time. Things were just fine, he said, there was nothing new — It looked like war — It looked like a bear market — It looked like Roosevelt — It looked like the Brooklyn Dodgers — It looked like rain and it was still hot. What kind of weather were they having at Winnisocket? What kind of a time was she having? What in the world were all those bills in her desk? She put the letter away in her bag and pensively began her orange juice. They were having perfect weather at Winnisocket — the air was like wine. Winnisocket, as the stationery said, was 'A Panoramic Playground with Everything to Play' and — well, she was playing.

She was playing golf — with Fred, who was so *glad* she'd arrived. Fred, known to the eight hundred or so guests of the Winnisocket House as 'Fwed,' was Mrs. Atterbury's best friend's nephew, age eighteen. 'Fwed' did not get along with people his own age. They didn't like him. Just what age did like him, Mrs. Cugat had come to wonder. He, however, liked her — tremendously. Too late, she discovered that she was the only person who'd given him a kind word in several years.

And she was playing tennis — with the brother of another of Mrs. Atterbury's friends — a man called The Commodore, who got along all right with his own age, but almost nobody else, being seventy-one and cross. He also liked her tremendously. This attachment, however, was looked upon by some of Mrs. Atterbury's friends with suspicion.

Also, due to a random game of quoits, she had become involved with the Activities Director, whose name was Russell. A gnarl of Activities had ensued — soft-ball, archery, shuffleboard, ping-pong, badminton, skeet shooting, fly casting, horseshoes, Bingo, bowling, bicycling and bridge —— She had judged a flower show, a dog show, and an Arthur Murray dance contest; reveled successively at a beach party, a masquerade, a gymkhana, and a concert in the Lounge; and sold cigarettes at a floor show sponsored by the Winnisocket Republican Committee, featuring Lawrence Tibbett — 'Fwed' and The Commodore dancing in jealous attendance throughout. She sighed.

The Winnisocket House swarmed with nice young people, but they were very young and stood up when she came into the room. There was an accumulation in every corner of nice old people, who twinkled and beamed at her over their needlepoint and newspapers, but appeared, tenderly, to consider her a child bride. There was also a tight little group of young married women, who lived in the cottages, and whose husbands came up for the week-ends. They played Mah-Jongg.

Mrs. Cugat had thought that this was her milieu and hopefully joined them once or twice, but she hadn't had much fun. They were just a little older than she; they were just enough older to feel at once envious and superior and, of course, they took it out on her. They said she mustn't let them bore her, after the excitements of the 'younger set,' and then talked about their children. Most of Mrs. Cugat's friends at home talked about their children too, but they seemed to have fewer children. These women, a step ahead of Mrs. Cugat's friends, had progressed to broods. They talked indignantly, over the tiles, of camps and dentists, despairingly of entrance examinations and clothes, archly of adolescence and gruesomely of impetigo. They also, Mrs. Cugat discovered, suspected that there was something 'pretty funny' about her and Mr. Cugat, else why was he not coming up?

But sticking demurely to Mrs. Atterbury and her two friends also had its disadvantages. When Mrs. Atterbury and her two friends weren't taking the whole day to motor to some distant tea-room to eat an enormous lunch, they were buying things. Expensive things — linens and their next winter's Christmas presents and old English silver — principally linens. Mrs. Cugat had been along on one or two of these forays and her American Express check-book looked like an old overshoe. Mr. Cugat was going to have to be written about this before she went home or she'd ride day-coach.

The week-end, however, might be more fun, she thought, and smiled a brave good morning over at The Commodore, who had just steamed into the dining-room and was being fussily berthed by the head-waiter and two captains. Husbands came up for the week-end. The sight of just a husband would be lovely — these downy young gods and courtly old satyrs! And, of course, one of the husbands might bring a friend — she hadn't quite given up on Anthony Eden and the small adventure.

The head-waiter arrived bearing a peach. 'With The Commodore's compliments,' he said. She bit into it stoically and idly scanned the Program of Events which was propped against the salt cellars. There was going to be a Surprise Tomorrow Night in the Ballroom at Nine O'Clock, it said. 'Fwed' had her for this, whatever it was — that Russell had yet an unplayed card seemed incredible.

But he had. Arriving there on the following night, they were just in time to hear his peculiarly rallying voice trumpet, 'Every lady draw a number — we're off to a Treasure Hunt!' The reason for drawing a number, it developed, to 'Fwed's' dismay, was to determine who your partner for the Treasure Hunt was to be. Gentlemen and ladies drew correspond-

ing numbers and then matched them up. Mrs.
Cugat drew resolutely and Russell bawled, 'Number
one-seventy! gentlemen, *one — seven — O*,' and held
it high over his head. She looked the room over —
the Saturday night crowd was certainly an improve-
ment on the week-night crowd — the Mah-Jongg
players and their husbands were all there and making a great deal of laughing to-do over matching
their numbers. They'd come in together from a
dinner party somewhere — jolly and intimate —
and she felt a sharp twinge of envy. The husbands
looked very nice — handsome and cheerful, reliable.
How lovely to have one there, she thought, all idea
of small adventure drowned in a wash of loneliness.

It would be such a comfort to talk to just an under-standing husband — even somebody else's. If only she'd draw one!

'Here I am, Beautiful,' said one of the hand-somest, cheerfulest, most unreliable-looking hus-bands she had ever seen, coming smilingly to meet her through the crowd. 'One-Seventy and all yours!' He belonged, as a matter of fact, to a little Mrs. Schroeder.

Little Mrs. Schroeder was slight and pathetic and rather desperately mothered one of the larger broods. She had a way of wearily brushing a limp and ever-present lock of hair off her forehead with the back of her hand while she told you about it. People usually referred to her as 'poor' little Mrs. Schroeder. One-Seventy they referred to as 'Prince Charlie.' He was a portrait painter. What's more, he looked like one. He had on a corduroy jacket. (Mr. Cugat, for instance, who was a banker, would never wear a corduroy jacket, Mrs. Cugat reflected.) He did not look the least bit like Anthony Eden, but he was, nevertheless, away over par — tall, stalwart and gray at the temples. Decorously, however, she tried not to appear too pleased — or, even to herself, admit beguilement; after all, a small adventure with somebody else's husband was no part of her plans. And particularly the husband of that *poor* little Mrs. Schroeder!

'Holy Mary! Look what I drew!' he marveled, delightedly and without scruple. 'I couldn't be more pleased!'

It was immediately apparent, however, that there were others who were not. Mrs. Cugat, quite evidently, was in possession of stolen goods.

'Don't you and Mrs. Cugat want to go with us, Chuck?' coaxed a wistful lady, who had drawn her own brother-in-law. 'We've plenty of room.'

'Charlie, remember what you promised this morning!' whispered another.

'They're going with us,' a third put in serenely. 'I've spoken to Pansy and it's all arranged.'

Someone else muttered cryptically, 'If I know Pansy, she'll take them herself!' and 'Fwed' exclaimed, in an incredulous and perfectly audible voice, 'You're not giving me the pitch for *that* heel!'

One-Seventy looked straight through him. 'Come, *cara mia*,' he said equably, 'let's get the hell out of here!' and throwing a backward and airy kiss, swept her through the door.

'Where's your car?' he asked practically as they emerged into the night.

Mrs. Cugat, a little rattled, was wondering about the Atterburys' station wagon. She had been driving it all week, but Mrs. Atterbury, pushing ever farther afield in her quest for new tea-rooms, had left that morning, with The Commodore's sister, for a two days' jaunt to the other side of the state. She felt a little guilty about taking it without permission and she felt a little guilty about 'poor' little Pansy, but she couldn't help feeling pleased at having escaped with something apparently coveted by every Mah-Jongg player. And no wonder, she thought, looking at him again.

'I've got a station wagon,' she said.

'Perfect, pet,' he replied. 'Lead on.'

'Where to?' she asked five minutes later, steering carefully out into the main highway. 'What's the first clue say?'

One-Seventy had stretched his long length out beside her and tipped his head comfortably onto the back of the seat. 'I don't know,' he sighed. 'What a relief to get away from those sheep!' Then he sat up, turned and smiled down into her eyes. 'You're different, though, aren't you, *dulce?*' he murmured, and leaned over and kissed her capably.

The station wagon came to a coughing halt. I've got to put a stop to this *right away*, she thought, with surprisingly little conviction.

'Sorry,' he said, recumbent again and in a matter-of-fact tone. 'That just came over me suddenly. Would you mind terribly if we didn't go on this Treasure Hunt?'

'Oh, but we must!' she exclaimed.

'No,' he said, 'we could go to the circus.'

'The circus?'

'Yes, there's a lovely one over on the east shore, sort of a carnival; it's been there all summer. I go often — just to get away from this mishmash' — he indicated Winnisocket's Panoramic Playground with a weary wave of the hand. 'I have to escape once in a while, you see, and mingle with just people — laugh with them, quarrel with them, cry with them — breathe dust and sweat — study types. I'm a painter, you know,' he added modestly. Mrs. Cugat, still hunting her breath, said Yes, she knew. 'And they have a very good roller-coaster,' he added.

'They have?' she managed more normally.

'Absolutely, the best. Anyway, nobody's going to run all over the countryside and get wet feet looking for Russell's bottle of American champagne — that's what the treasure always is; he's been having these for years. We just buy a bottle and bring it back — everybody does.'

'Can I go on the roller-coaster as many times as I want to?' she asked, sparring for time.

'You can stay on till it closes, child. I have a pass. Let's get going!'

On the drive over, Mrs. Cugat, from time to time, endeavored to make her conscience wrestle, but it remained curiously inert. She began to wonder if she had one. It was awful of them to duck out of the Treasure Hunt this way, she prodded it anxiously; people would talk. But people *always* talked. They were even talking about her and The Commodore, and did that bother her? No. Why, then, should this? She and One-Seventy were only going to the circus, and if he tried to kiss her again, she would just stop him.

But he did not try again. He said, 'Tell me about yourself, angel,' and immediately launched off into a high-flavored tale of himself and Clifton Fadiman. She endeavored, in turn, to put in a word or two about Mr. Cugat, but he got off again onto himself and Howard Hughes and then onto himself and, inevitably, Harpo Marx. It was all entrancing, though — she felt in actual touch with the world of Winchell; as far as she was concerned, they arrived at the circus, roller-coaster or no roller-coaster, far too soon. Regretfully she brought the station wagon to a halt in a little grove of trees.

'Why, here we are!' he said, and sat up briskly and put on his hat. Then he turned, looked at her a moment, and took it off again. Leaning over, he cupped her face in his hands. ' "*A lovely being, scarcely formed or molded,*" ' he whispered. "*A rose, with all its sweetest leaves yet folded.*" '

Mrs. Cugat winced. There was something about recited poetry. Mr. Cugat, of course, never — still, she *must* get over this stuffy habit of judging all men by Mr. Cugat!

'George Gordon, Lord Byron,' said One-Seventy, rescuing the moment deftly and releasing her face; then he opened the door and jumped lightly to the ground. 'Now for a little revelry!'

Inside, however, he had another change of mood — he seemed suddenly preoccupied and his eyes, under knitted brows, ransacked the crowd. Studying types, thought Mrs. Cugat, somewhat disappointed but nevertheless interested. They wandered up and down aimlessly, but he seemed to have forgotten all about the roller-coaster.

'Here's a shooting gallery,' she said timidly, wondering if she should have spoken. 'Do you like to shoot?'

'I loathe it,' he said briefly. Then he turned and said, suddenly interested, 'Do you like it?'

Mrs. Cugat was quite a good shot and, justifiably, rather proud of it. She had been captain of the rifle team for three summers at camp. 'Yes, I do,' she said, hoping to recapture admiration, 'quite a lot.'

'There's a little rider here, with the Wild West Show, named Ida,' he said surprisingly. 'I'd like to have you meet her. Suppose you plink away at those bunnies while I go look her up.'

Mrs. Cugat felt rather damped, but there seemed

nothing to do but agree smilingly. 'I won't be a moment,' he said in a suddenly lightened tone and, handing her a dollar, was gone. She picked up a gun.

Slightly out of humor, her eye was deadly; a parade of twenty-four rabbits and twenty-four ducks went down to death without a miss.

'Say, *Lady!*' the proprietor exclaimed in admiration. Mrs. Cugat raised another gun and knocked off twelve small marching men. She felt better. An interested and approving audience gathered; more joined it. Before she knew it, she had won a bridge lamp. The crowd applauded and several congratulated her. Where, though, she wondered anxiously, amid her triumph, were One-Seventy and Ida?

'Are you the lady from the hotel?' inquired a voice behind her, and she turned to discover a resplendently appareled cowboy with a six-shooter riding each hip. His face, however, between the scarlet silk of his neckerchief and the creamy felt of his fabulous hat, wore the severity of a young Jesuit. He removed one of the six-shooters, turned and thoughtfully emptied it, with deadly effect, into the parade of rabbits.

'Now, Les,' the proprietor expostulated, 'if you've shot them rabbits full of holes again, you'll have to pay plenty!' But the cowboy paid him no heed.

'Did you come here tonight with a rattlesnake named Charlie Schroeder?' he inquired of Mrs. Cugat casually.

'Why, yes,' she gulped, and then, alarmed, quavered, 'Why, where is he?'

He put the gun back in its holster, picked up the bridge lamp and offered his arm. 'When I last saw him,' he said boredly, 'he was making far-apart tracks for the woods. Can you get home all right?'

Mrs. Cugat took his arm dazedly and they walked toward the gate; halfway there, however, her brain started working again. 'Look here!' she said, dropping the arm abruptly. 'I want to know what's happened. Where is Mr. Schroeder? What have you done to him?'

He smiled faintly for the first time. 'Don't worry,' he said kindly; 'he ain't hurt — only a little spooked up. I tore up some earth at his feet with my six-gun and he stampeded.'

Mrs. Cugat's reactions to this *contretemps* were chaotic. Still frightened, she wanted, nevertheless, to laugh. Suave, imperturbable One-Seventy spooked up and stampeding!

'But why?' she queried, groping for reality. 'What did he do?'

The cowboy sobered again. 'He was hanging around my little sister Ida again,' he said sternly. 'I warned him last week, but I guess the old tomcat didn't believe me.'

'Oh,' said Mrs. Cugat. She climbed into the station wagon and he set the bridge lamp carefully in beside her.

'Ida's a soft-boiled bo-peep,' he said resignedly. 'She'll fall for anything. I thought it was about time to shoo this Romeo off — he'd started working in poetry. He says she's *"A rosebud set with little wilful thorns,"*' he quoted sourly, *"and sweet as"* Idaho *"air could make her."*'

'George Gordon, Lord Byron?' ventured Mrs. Cugat.

'Alfred, Lord Tennyson, I believe,' he replied shortly. 'Well, take care of yourself.'

'Oh, thank you, I will,' she replied, awed.

On the seat beside her, One-Seventy's hat reposed unaware. She lifted it daintily by two fingers
and dropped it out the window. It rolled over on
its back in the dust. Then, ashamed, she got out
and retrieved it. After all, this was no time to be
childish — he'd been shot at, perhaps wounded!
Someone ought to be told. But she didn't know
who — and after all, why should she bother? He'd
left her cold to go off and dally with soft-boiled Ida
from Idaho, hadn't he? She picked up the hat and
dropped it out the window again. Then she blew
her nose, jammed the station wagon into gear, and
backed it hard into a tree.

The ride back to the Winnisocket House was long,
bitter, and creaking; the elevator boy, she thought,
when she finally reached there, looked at her oddly;
when she got to the door of her room, she found she
was carrying the bridge lamp.

'That'll be just forty dollars,' the village garage-
man said next morning, carefully toting up projected repairs to the station wagon.

'You can't make it any less?' Mrs. Cugat asked,
without hope.

'Not if you want it by tomorrow night, I can't;
I'm gonna have to put three men on it to get it
done.'

'Well, it's got to be ready by then,' she said unhappily, and signed and tore out her last two Express checks. If only Mrs. Atterbury would stay away one more day — there'd been some talk of it. The back of the station wagon was caved in like a paper box. Perhaps there was a telegram from her at the post office. Folding the checkbook's empty covers, she started walking back along the road to Winnisocket. She had exactly one dollar and twenty cents left. Maybe the linen man would take back that largest luncheon set and refund cash. He had looked kindly. She couldn't bear to wire Mr. Cugat. Her conscience, so perversely dormant the night before, had a half-Nelson on her this morning. He'd been thoughtful and generous, as always, and what had she done the moment she'd got off alone? Thrown his money away, smashed up his employer's car, and let a portrait painter kiss her. She ought to have a nurse. Darling Mr. Cugat! A lump rose in her throat; if only he were here so she could tell him all about it! Trouble borne alone weighed so heavy. Or could she tell him? That corduroy jacket might not go down ——

She turned up a path that was a short cut to the post office and came out of the woods at the back of the building. A hum from the front porch proclaimed the usual gathering there awaiting the mail. Coming along the side of the building under its open windows, she was just in time to hear somebody say, '*Good* morning, all! Anything exciting happen last night?' and a delighted feminine chorus reply, 'Pa-*lenty!*' She stopped dead in her tracks.

'Poor little Pansy,' one voice went on with relish, 'has just been put to bed and the doctor ordered — Bonnie Prince Charlie got home from the Treasure Hunt at *seven o'clock* this morning!'

'My dear!' There was a breathless pause, and then, 'Who was he with this time?'

'The little blonde divorcée from the hotel!'

'Oh!'

Mrs. Cugat turned to flee. Then she halted uncertainly, hot with anger. She must get hold of herself. The only thing to do was to brazen it out and explain. It would never do to let that story grow. Divorcée! Those old cats! — any one of them would have given their eye teeth last night to have drawn Bonnie Charlie. She powdered her nose and stepped around the corner of the building and up the steps, her head high — to be greeted by a shriek. Out of the door of the post office came Mrs. Atterbury's friend, the aunt of 'Fwed,' flanked by agitated supporters. Catching sight of Mrs. Cugat, however, she flung them aside and stepped forward unaided.

'You!' she cried in a shaking voice. 'See what you've done!' and shoved an opened letter into Mrs. Cugat's limp hand.

Mrs. Cugat glanced at it and then looked again

— 'Fwed' had gone to join the Navy, having discovered, he said, that the woman he loved was only playing with him. Minute directions followed for the disposal of his belongings. Forgivingly, he had left Mrs. Cugat all his victrola records. She handed the letter back without a word and quietly turned and went down the steps.

'Will you make a reservation on the first train for Albany?' she said to the hotel porter. 'I can have my things ready in half an hour.'

The taxi jolted along familiar maple-shaded streets, quiet in the heat. How perfectly lovely, she thought happily, clasping her bag, not to have the air like wine. How perfectly lovely to be home! It was funny, though, that Mr. Cugat hadn't met her at the station; she had wired him — with money from the linen man, who had refused to take back the largest luncheon set, but had kindly lent her ten dollars. The taxi drew up at the house and she got out eagerly. In the driveway was a perfectly strange yellow roadster — with a pink satin bathing-suit hung over one of its doors. Staring, she went up the walk and rang the bell. Who in the world did that car belong to? Then she turned — an impassive Filipino in a white coat was at the door.

'Do the Cugats live here?' she stammered with the impact of the surprise.

'Come in, come in, come in,' he replied in a weary tone and, opening the screen, admitted her and took her bag.

She stepped into her own front hall uncertainly. Filipino and bag vanished. From the library came the rippling strains of somebody whistling '*Nola*.' On tiptoe, she crossed the hall and peeped timidly into the room; the walls were red instead of blue and a man was painting the ceiling.

'The folks are in the solarium,' he said, without looking down, and resumed his whistling. Mrs. Cugat turned and put a shaking hand out to the wall for support. Strange laughter floated from the sun-porch. Reaching it somehow, she found four people — three girls in dark glasses and a man with his hat on — playing bridge. All looked up with no surprise, and one said pleasantly, 'The drinks are in the pantry, dear; and bring some ice back, will you?'

In the pantry, however, on the sink, sat a figure of more or less reality — Mr. Cory Cartwright, dressed in tennis shoes, evening trousers, and a pajama coat. He was eating two fried eggs on a piece of bread.

'Hello, Liz,' he said affably. 'Just get in?'

'Cory!' she cried, her voice shrill with relief. 'What's happened? What are you doing here? Where's George? Where's Anna?'

Mr. Cartwright looked at her owlishly and she saw that he was none too sober. He took a bite and chewed it deliberately. 'Anna —— ' he said, concentrating intently. 'My word! Don't you know about *Anna?*'

'No, I don't! What's happened to her?'

He took another bite and shook his head. 'Her sister's oldest girl got a tumor. Anna had to go home,' he said. Then he went on, swallowing: 'But it's all right, we got Suki from the club. You remember old Suki — used to look after George and me? Or — maybe you don't —— '

Mrs. Cugat was staring frightened and wide-eyed through the kitchen door; a trained nurse was bustling back and forth there, preparing a tray.

Cory leaned far forward anxiously and only just recovered himself. 'Oh, that,' he said relievedly, back on the sink. 'That's only Miss Heffelfinger: she takes care of Bill. You know, Liz, poor Bill, living down there at the club all the time with no home life or anything, gets into pretty bad shape once in a while — Heffelfinger's the only one who can bring him out of it. Old George thought, in all this heat, it might be pleasanter for them out here — country air and all ——'

'Do you mean to tell me that that horrible Bill Stone has been having his DTs all over *my* house?' Mrs. Cugat exploded.

'Now, Liz,' he said placatingly, 'we got him tied.'

'And who,' she asked icily, 'are the young things on the sun-porch?'

'Oh, those ——' Cory looked pained. 'Well, I suppose you remember Lola?'

'Lola who? Your niece?'

'Yes. Well, Lola fell in love down at the boat-races and got carried away and asked everybody in New London to the wedding. Only the crews and cheering sections came, but Mother ran out of beds, so old George offered to take some in. Wonderful of him, I must say — the brats have been lively.'

'And the library?'

'Yes. One went to sleep in the tub upstairs with the water running — college boys do that, you know. I picked out the new wallpaper. Do you like it? Nice warm color, I thought. Old George wasn't so sure ——'

'And where,' she said, 'is hospitable old George?'

'Where is he?' Cory stammered blankly. Then he said, 'Oh, my goodness!'

Mrs. Cugat chilled. 'What do you mean, "Oh my goodness!" ?'

Cory looked at her solemnly. 'Liz, honey,' he said, 'he's gotten awful weak ——'

'Well?'

'The big softie bowed out last night and grabbed a plane for Winnisocket!'

. . . worldly goods . . .

'MINK COATS only nine-fifty,' said Mrs. Cugat, rattling her *New York Times* overtly. Mr. Cugat, in his chair on the opposite side of the fireplace, remained immersed in *Tax Liability Reviewed in the Light of Recent Developments.*

'Eastern mink coats, only thirteen-seventy-five,' she continued, a little louder. Mr. Cugat turned a page.

'Labrador mink, dark-bluish pelts, luxurious cape collar, three-quarter length, nipped-in waist — two thousand.'

'What d'ya know,' muttered Mr. Cugat. 'No income results unless deduction in prior year has reduced liability!'

Mrs. Cugat lowered the *New York Times.* 'Two thousand is pretty reasonable, I think,' she said, in the slightly raised tone and level inflection kept for the very deaf.

'What?' he asked politely, coming out from behind his review. 'What were you saying?'

'I was just reading about a sale of mink coats,' she began all over again, undaunted. 'I said I thought two thousand dollars was pretty reasonable, don't you?'

'Something's reasonable at two thousand dollars?' asked Mr. Cugat.

'A mink coat,' said Mrs. Cugat patiently. 'There *are* cheaper ones, of course,' she admitted, 'but this one is natural Labrador, bluish pelts, and three-quarter length.'

'Let's see it,' said Mr. Cugat in incredulous tones.

Before he could even get his glasses out, she had got the *Times* whisked deftly over on top of *Tax Liability Reviewed in the Light of Recent Developments* and smoothed out to advantage. Mr. Cugat scanned the page intently. He looked 'cute' — she always thought — in his glasses, but he seldom used them, having stubbornly held, since the day he got them, that they were no damned good. He did, however, employ them occasionally to create an impression of judicial consideration. He was using them to create that impression now.

'This one,' she said, pointing eagerly.

Mr. Cugat peered at it intently. 'Blue?' he queried.

'Oh George, stop being dense! Of course it isn't

blue. You know perfectly well what mink looks like. Good Lord!'

'Oh, those *brown* furs everybody's got! I don't like them — too common.'

'Darling, that's just like saying you don't like — diamonds — because they're common! You just sound silly. There's something *about* mink!'

'I like gray fur,' he said surprisingly. 'What's that fluffy gray fur coat that Peggy Marvin wears? I like that — it looks swell.'

'Oh George, it doesn't either — it's opossum. Nobody but a schoolgirl wears opossum.'

'Peggy does,' he maintained stoutly.

'Peggy's had that coat ever since she was in college,' sputtered Mrs. Cugat, 'just because Twitch Marvin's too tight to buy her a suitable one!'

'It must *wear* pretty well,' said Mr. Cugat interestedly. Then he added, peering through his glasses at the mink again, 'But you wouldn't want one, huh?'

'No, I wouldn't! My own Persian lamb jacket's nicer than opossum.'

'You look so pretty in gray too,' said Mr. Cugat regretfully. 'I remember when I used to come home from school for vacations and go to church with Aunt Edith — you'd always come in with your mother, dressed all up in a gray fur coat and a little round hat, and I thought you were the cutest trick there. Of course, your mouth was all full of braces and elastic bands and things and your legs were pretty skinny, but I used to sit there, overlooking every drawback, and plan to marry you anyway. The hat had earmuffs,' he added.

'Why, darling!' she gasped, almost overcome by the sweet surprise of this revelation. 'Why haven't you ever told me that before!'

'Haven't thought of it since,' explained Mr. Cugat reasonably. 'Wouldn't you like another gray coat like that one — or was it opossum too?'

'Worse,' said Mrs. Cugat. 'It was gray squirrel. Nobody but an infant wears gray squirrel.'

But she had lost interest for the moment even in mink coats. She shoved both the *New York Times* and *Tax Liability Reviewed in the Light of Recent Developments* off onto the floor and clambered into her husband's lap to snuggle down and give herself up to dreamy thoughts of faraway Sundays at church in her gray squirrel coat.

Why, that must have been ages before she even went away to school! If she had had any idea then that that sort of 'wild'-looking George Cugat (here she burrowed possessively deep into Mr. Cugat's lap), who occasionally visited his aunt for vacations and was a senior at Yale, was sitting there behind her and planning, in spite of her braces and her legs, to marry her — well, she would probably have

dropped dead. The idea, fortunately, had not occurred to her; she had sat through church every Sunday all that winter, pleasantly occupied in inventing a romance between herself and the dark, second-from-the-left bass chorister, whose wife, standing unaware, among the altos, had been summarily disposed of in the first installment.

'These pants were pressed just yesterday,' Mr. Cugat broke in tentatively.

Several days later he called her from the office. 'I have to go to New York on business for the old man,' he said. 'Would you like to go along? You could get some of your Christmas shopping done while I'm busy.'

'Oh yes,' she breathed.

'Can you be ready to leave tomorrow?' he asked.

'I have to get there right away to entertain some big shot for him — he's got asthma again and can't go. It doesn't give you much time to get your dresses and things ready, but I thought you might manage ——'

'Oh I'll manage all right,' she assured him, and hanging up the receiver sped in all haste to her mother's.

That lady was discovered daintily but efficiently potting bulbs in her greenhouse. 'Have you anything fit to take?' she inquired practically when she'd been breathlessly told.

'Well, I have my suit with the Persian lamb jacket for daytimes, and for dinner I have my black-and-gold and that print you gave me last summer,' Mrs. Cugat proffered anxiously.

'You can't wear a last summer's print in New York in December,' her mother said decidedly. 'But Max has a bottle-green velvet in his window with silver leaves that will be just right. I'll give it to you,' she smiled. 'You'll have to make an impression on George's big shot, certainly.'

Mrs. Cugat jumped for joy. 'Will Max get it altered in time?' she worried.

'I'll tell him,' said her mother firmly. 'He will. Now, run right down there before lunch and then make an appointment for your hair, and be sure to see that your shoes and gloves are nice.'

Mrs. Cugat sobered suddenly. 'If I *only* had a mink coat,' she sighed.

'Maybe you will some day,' her mother said lightly. 'Meanwhile that red tweed evening coat with the frogs is very young and smart. I wouldn't worry about myself for a minute in that.' She took hold of Mrs. Cugat's chin and, turning up her face, scrutinized it closely — to see if it was clean, presumably — she'd been doing this since Mrs. Cugat was three. Then she added, 'Would you like to borrow my silver-fox cape?'

Mrs. Cugat was borne down to Max's on the wings of rapture.

New York at Christmas time is exciting. Everything is so dazzlingly dressed. Little store windows are like lighted jewel cases — big store windows are each a spectacle — avenues are garlanded — buildings are bedizened, and in the theaters the actors play to audiences of eager, responsive young faces and all-night orchestras play to eager, responsive young feet. It's the height of the season, Christmas is coming and school is out! Amid all this at the St. Regis — in one of the very best suites — sat Mr. and Mrs. Cugat eating chicken hash for breakfast at the expense of the firm.

'Did you ever *have* so much fun!' she said dreamily. 'I feel like a billionairess.'

'Don't get the habit,' cautioned Mr. Cugat abstractedly, checking over a long list.

'Now, darling, stop worrying about that list,' she expostulated. 'Everything's done and going to be lovely. All the people you tried to get can come, the theater tickets are for an opening, I spent an hour with the head-waiter over the hors d'oeuvres and half an hour with the florist; you found the wine you wanted and got the table you asked for. There's not a single thing left to be done. This afternoon we'll just relax and go look in windows.'

Mr. Cugat toyed absently with his hash, but was finally persuaded out, and they strode briskly uptown and then, after lunch, loitered leisurely down

— looking in windows. Mink was everywhere — displayed in still beauty — surging up and down the sidewalks.

'Look at that one!' exclaimed Mrs. Cugat, tugging Mr. Cugat back to a small arched window, hung in gray velvet and containing nothing but a big silver box, from which spilled more, amid a froth of star-splashed tissue.

'Looks like all the rest of 'em to me,' said Mr. Cugat boredly. 'Why on earth you want one of those! You don't wear much brown, do you?'

'Oh George,' she sighed, exasperated. 'It isn't just something *brown* — it's *mink* — mink's different!'

'Different! That's good.' He laughed heartily. 'I'll bet you a champagne cocktail in at the Ritz that I can count ten minks right from here with one eye shut.'

'All the more reason why I should have one,' said Mrs. Cugat crossly; 'and I mean to some day.'

'It won't be my money pays for it,' retorted Mr. Cugat sharply, keyed to an unusual pitch by other responsibilities. And if it hadn't been for the champagne cocktail (which Mr. Cugat's money *did* pay for — there being only eight minks in sight at the time he counted), relations might have become strained. As it was, they drank their cocktails up and an involuntary truce was declared.

Back at the St. Regis, however, Mrs. Cugat, in her bath, was again fretted by righteous indignation. Apparently Mr. Cugat was perfectly able and willing to give her a new fur coat for Christmas; not once had he pleaded economy — it was just that he didn't like mink. It was just that he didn't understand mink, that was all. Somehow he'd have to be shown.

Mrs. Cugat did much of her most brilliant thinking in the bathtub, and now, amid vapors of Yardley's Lavender, a brilliant plan emerged. It was not an infallible, but certainly a worth-trying, plan for showing Mr. Cugat. It required, however, an almost insuperable sacrifice on her part. From all she had heard of tonight's assemblage it was a pretty safe guess that mink would be manifest. She, in her mother's silver-fox cape, of course, would hold her own nicely and be a credit to Mr. Cugat — which he'd take entirely for granted, but if she wore the red tweed evening coat — brought along for no particular reason and probably good and mussy by now, having been relegated to the back of the trunk — she'd stand out like the poor little matchgirl. Her humble state would thus be brought to his notice and he might be jarred into some realization of mink's prestige. She had a fleeting moment of loyalty to Mr. Atterbury and the firm, but brushed it aside — her own mother had said that the red

tweed was smart, and it was. However, she concluded, it might be a little more sporting to have it
pressed.

Resolve wavered all the time she was dressing,
but she managed to bolster it valiantly, although a
sneak view in the bathroom mirror of the bottle-
green velvet in combination with the silver fox nearly
broke her heart. Bravely, however, she hid the cape
away again — and laying out the hurriedly pressed
tweed went to join Mr. Cugat, who was looking
lovely in tails and nervously pacing back and forth
in the parlor.

'Remember, now,' he instructed her earnestly,
'T. J. Smith is the big noise in this affair and he's
the only one I don't know. They're all pretty important to the old man, of course, but sort of concentrate on the Smiths.'

'Concentrate on the Smiths,' repeated Mrs. Cugat
dutifully, and there was a knock at the door.

The first arrivals — Mrs. Cugat went forward to
meet them brimming with gratefulness — were two
pairs of feminine shoulders literally bowed by mink.
That cape's a little on the light side, she thought
critically, but there it was — mink and lots of it.
The next elevator brought a swagger, a dolman, and
a stole — with a matching muff like a mattress.
Mrs. Cugat, delighted with the success of her plan,
sparkled. Mr. Cugat was urbane and charming.

It was a full half-hour, however, before the T. J. Smiths arrived. They entered graciously — like royalty. T. J. was surprisingly young and strangely unattractive — he was sort of shiny and had light eyes. Mrs. T. J. was French or something.

Mr. Cugat looked at T. J. intently. 'Hey,' he said suddenly, 'you were in my class at Hotchkiss!'

Mrs. Cugat looked at Mrs. T. J. and then looked away again. Mrs. T. J., trim, vivacious, and with bangs, was dressed all in gray — her coat a fluffy fox jacket.

Mr. Cugat did not again refer to Hotchkiss, but he treated T. J., along with champagne and creamed oysters, to more soft soap than Mrs. Cugat could believe possible of him. Mrs. T. J. he treated differently; his eyes crinkled in appreciation every time he looked at her. That damned fox jacket! Her lovely plan had completely flopped. The minks, gathering their wraps about them in sumptuous homogeneity, as they prepared to leave for the theater, looked like a Greek chorus. Mrs. T. J., gesticulating, in her fox jacket looked as cute as a bug's ear. Mrs. Cugat hastily got out her mother's silver-fox cape again — one solace, no point now to red tweed.

The evening went off perfectly — the opening was brilliant and their supper superb. T. J.'s light eyes, under Mr. Cugat's blandishments, warily warmed. Mrs. T. J. shrugged and blew kisses and was perfectly charming. Mr. Cugat helped her on or off with the gray fox jacket no less, it seemed, than twenty times.

'Well,' said Mrs. Cugat, when they finally got back to their rooms, 'Mr. Atterbury ought to be very pleased and proud of you — everything went off beautifully, I thought.'

Mr. Cugat slung his best silk hat across the room, where it bounced off the wall and into the fireplace. Mrs. Cugat gaped at him in amazement.

'He'd better be proud of me,' he exploded. 'How I've kept from pushing that soap-face in all evening, I'll never know. Do you know who the great T. J. Smith *is?* None other than little school chum Sneaky Smith — known in his youth as Creeping Jemmy! Wait till I tell Cory! To think of a great

guy like Atterbury playing up to that — !' Then he quieted down a little and added, 'His wife looked cute, though, didn't she?'

Just as if opening nights, rose-filled suites, champagne cocktails, and silver-fox capes had never been, scarcely thirty-six hours later found Mr. and Mrs. Cugat back again at their own fireside — Mrs. Cugat reading the *New York Times*, Mr. Cugat perusing *The Business and Legislation Report of the Research Institute of America, Inc.*

'Only sixteen hundred,' Mrs. Cugat said softly, with a hopeless little sigh.

Mr. Cugat put down *The Business and Legislation Report of the Research Institute of America, Inc.*, and came over to lean on the back of her chair, his head close to hers. 'Climaxing Our Greatest Mink Season! Luxurious Natural or Tipped Mink Coats, Wild or Ranch, Canadian, Russian, or Eastern,' he read. Then he said gently, 'Still yearning, hmm?'

Mrs. Cugat nodded wistfully and he rumpled up her hair. 'Keep at it,' he said. 'Hunger breaks down stone walls.'

She speculated upon this maxim with growing excitement for the rest of the evening. What did he mean? Had he finally succumbed? Was he actually planning to give her a *mink coat* for Christmas? Or was he just teasing her? Could he afford a mink

coat? queried Prudence, in a small voice, rushing
belatedly to the fore, with the incredible entrance
of *mink* into the realm of possibility. She could
hardly go to sleep.

The next morning she left a brief kiss for Mr.
Cugat on the top of his head, as he sat, finishing his
coffee, at breakfast. 'I've got a thousand things to
do,' she explained hurriedly and with a shining face.
'My presents have to be delivered today and half
of them aren't wrapped. Don't forget to go down
to the wholesale place and pick out the tree and
have that string of lights fixed — I've left it on the
hall table.' Christmas to Mrs. Cugat had endured
not one whit less enchanting than when she was
twelve.

'OK,' said Mr. Cugat, leisurely pouring himself
yet another cup of coffee. 'Get about your business.'

Mrs. Cugat sped to the guest room, where piles
of boxes, bright wrappings, excelsior, scissors,
stickers, cards, and shining ribbon strewed its prim
formality. Unfolding a card table she placed it in
front of the window and sat down, humming — with
eight small boxes to be wrapped in a paper that
looked like hand-tooled white leather and tied with
a thin gold cord with tasseled ends. These were for
the Luncheon Club and she was very pleased with
them — the wrapping she had found the last minute
at a very smart shop in New York; none of the

Luncheon Club, she was quite sure, would have ever seen anything like it; and the presents were pretty nice too — little gilt stamp boxes, each monogrammed. She was holding one off at arm's length in admiration, when her eye strayed to the window. Mr. Cugat, below, was struggling with the garage doors and awkwardly juggling a perfectly huge package. A package wrapped in heavy brown paper and the cord sealed with little blobs of lead. A fur-coat box, surely! But where was he taking it? And where had he had it all this time? She was so excited she could hardly finish the presents, and finally, unable to contain herself, went down to the kitchen to see what Anna thought. Anna, however, obviously bought, wasn't telling.

Christmas Day dawned at last and the sun, blazing doubly bright over fresh snow into the Cugats' dining-room window, lit a festive scene. A moth-eaten and somewhat tawdry-looking little tree, which Mr. Cugat had had since childhood and which he refused to have refurbished or eat Christmas breakfast without, revolved at breakneck speed in the center of the table caroling 'Hark! the Herald Angels Sing'; Anna, bearing kippers and creamed potatoes, trod proudly in and out wearing pearl earrings — from the night watchman; Lillian rolled with abandon in catnip; Mr. Cugat, between bites of his favorite breakfast, experimentally trained his new binoculars on the house across the street, and announced happily that he might as well be right in the same room with its occupants and that he believed that they all had hangovers. At the head of the table sat Mrs. Cugat, dreamily, eating nothing and robed in mink — natural Labrador, full-length, bluish pelts.

'Darling, are you sure you can afford it?' she asked anxiously, when the effects of the first shock had finally worn off and she had been made to sip a little coffee.

'Sure,' said Mr. Cugat, getting up and pinching her cheek. 'I dipped into a little fund I keep for trips or emergencies. It's looking a little poorly at the moment, but maybe we'll strike oil before it's time for Bermuda again.'

'Oh dearest!' cried Mrs. Cugat. 'You gave up your beloved Bermuda trip just for me!'

'Not entirely,' said Mr. Cugat, returning interestedly to the family across the street.

In due time the telephone began to ring. 'The Luncheon Club,' he observed, 'checking up to see who's ahead.'

Mrs. Cugat flew upstairs to the phone. It was Susie Wagoner. 'Liz, darling,' she said, 'your present was adorable. I never saw anything cuter.'

'I loved yours too,' said Mrs. Cugat, 'just what I

needed most,' and waited breathlessly for the next
question.

'What'd George give you?' asked Mrs. Wagoner
with gratifying promptness.

'A mink coat,' said Mrs. Cugat, bending every
effort to sound casual. 'It's really a sweet one. I'm
so pleased.'

'Oh, mink,' said Mrs. Wagoner. 'How nice — you
heard, of course, what Howie gave Evie?'

'No, what?' asked Mrs. Cugat.

'A platinum-fox jacket!' Mrs. Wagoner breathed.
'There're only about three in the country, you
know.'

'That was last year,' said Mrs. Cugat, and then,
recollecting herself, exclaimed, 'How *simply* divine!'

Mrs. Blake called next. 'Mink?' she said when
the preliminaries were over. 'How nice, my dear —
you've wanted one for so *long!* You've heard, of
course, what Howie gave Evie?'

'So George gave you a mink coat,' caroled Mrs.
Taylor, hard on the heels of Mrs. Blake. 'My dear,
you'll never regret it for a minute — I found mine
so practical, I just bought another for sport. You
heard, of course, what Howie gave Evie?'

The telephone continued to ring. Mrs. Cugat
examined an impulse to call Peggy Marvin of the
college opossum, who lived away out in the country
with a long-distance phone and so perhaps had not

yet heard of platinum fox. Genuine kind-hearted-
ness stopped her — Twitch Marvin had probably
given poor Peggy some new shrubbery for Christmas — or had a humidifier installed. Platinum fox
— she wasn't very sure she knew what it looked like.
One of the ten best-dressed women in the world had
some — they'd hear plenty about that — but who
cared what Evie Sturm had anyway — she usually
bought her own presents and then had to break
the news to Howie.

'Well, did everybody burn satisfactorily over your
coat?' asked Mr. Cugat pleasantly, when she came
downstairs again. He was already delicately taking
his new binoculars apart over by the window in a
good light. Mr. Cugat always took his Christmas
presents apart on Christmas morning if possible.

'I should say they did,' exclaimed Mrs. Cugat
grumpily. 'They could hardly wait to tell me that
Evie Sturm's got a *platinum-fox jacket.*'

'That's what I got you first,' said Mr. Cugat,
carefully inserting a tiny screwdriver in a minute
screw and beginning to turn it with care. 'Platinum
fox was what Sneaky Smith's wife's jacket was. I
liked it so well I asked him where he got it and how
much it was. I must say the price rocked me a bit,
but he acted so damned superior and "M'dear
fellow" that I said "Fine, Sneaky, that's just what
I want for my wife — come help me pick one out!"

So he did and, if I know him, he probably wangled a
commission. But then, after I got home, I came to
my senses and realized that I'd bought it for pretty
selfish reasons and mink was what you wanted, not
fox, so I changed it. I had a hell of a time doing it,
but it all turned out all right and I saved a little
money to boot. Although that's not an ordinary
mink coat, young lady,' he added proudly. 'I'll bet
there's not a better one in town.' He looked up at
her. 'You're not *sorry* I changed it, are you?'

Mrs. Cugat hastily pulled up her dropped jaw.
'I should say not,' she managed. 'Platinum fox!'
Then she got up, looked into the mirror, and added
stoutly, 'There's something *about* mink!'

...by joining hands...

MRS. CUGAT, in Scheherezade's shoes, would have had no trouble at all — *two* thousand and one nights wouldn't have stumped her; she was a natural spinner of tales. Added to an untrammeled imagination, she possessed a taste for detail, a cunning in adjectives and a mastery of climax. In fact, everyday incidents became polished to such brightness through her telling that, sometimes, they were barely recognizable; which, of course, was regrettable, for she was, basically, an honest person. It was just that such a lively talent was hard to hold and she occasionally got run away with. No one was more distressed when this happened than Mrs. Cugat herself, who, checked suddenly by realization, would become appalled, and set her nimble mind scurrying to devise plausibility. Doing this usually entailed several counterplots, so things were seldom bettered.

As distressed as Mrs. Cugat and much more un-
comfortable about it was Mr. Cugat, a bland and
rational creature, abashed and perplexed by what
was, to him, blatant romancing. Just at first he had
been inclined to take an indulgent view, deeming it
a small fault, sensitive to cure. 'Not the Northwest
Mounted, honey,' he'd interpolate quietly. 'He was
only a cop'; or, 'Ten *thousand* dollars, Liz, hardly ten
million!' But Mrs. Cugat, acceding meekly, would
seek immediate compensation in further artistry;
so, with the passing years, he had gradually abandoned censure and simply faced the fact that colorful anecdote was a part of her — like her unnatural
appetite for salted peanuts or her fondness for cats —
bizarre traits which were no part of him. He did
not excuse it, however; he merely concluded to himself, sadly, that there was a lack of moral fiber somewhere in her makeup and that, charming though
she was, lying must just come easy. He called it
'whiffling,' though — a nicer word.

The Town Hall lecture was just over; '*Ship me
somewhere east of Suez, Where the best is like the worst,
Where there aren't no Ten Commandments, An' a man can
raise a thirst!*' the bronzed young man on the platform had pleaded in conclusion, and Mrs. Cugat's
luncheon club, from their seats in the second row,
expelled a long sigh.

'Those wishing to have their copies of *Mad Dogs and Englishmen* autographed by Captain Allingham will form a line to the right,' announced the chairman, pitching her voice valiantly over the sound of scraping chairs. 'Luncheon will be served in the Pompeiian Room in one half-hour.'

Mrs. Cugat's luncheon club gathered together their coats and books and, to a woman, fell in line.

'Think of living all that time on hardtack and cucumbers!'

'Or paddling for three days upstream in a basket!'

'Or having to saw off your best friend's leg ——'

'And with a *nail file!*'

The line moved slowly up and past the bronzed young man, who smiled and signed his name over and over again without a variation in expression or chirography. Mrs. Cugat examined her still damp autograph pleasurably. 'I love the name Derek, don't you?' she said. 'It simply sounds intrepid — I can hardly wait to meet him.'

The luncheon club backed regretfully toward the Pompeiian Room. 'Some people have all the luck,' somebody grumbled. 'The time I was asked to sit at the speakers' table it was with Mickey Rooney.' Mrs. Cugat looked smug; so did her two close friends, Mrs. Sturm and Mrs. Wagoner. 'We'll tell you all about him, darlings,' they said airily. 'Excuse us now while we go powder up!'

The speakers' table was on a raised dais, loftily overlooking a thicket of smaller tables. At it, with Captain Derek Allingham, author-explorer, were seated nine select personages. There was 'that terribly interesting' Professor Wiggin from the University and a Miss Snell from the Book Department of Himmelhock, Ampers and Briggs and young Gerald Porter, who had graduated from Yale, been around the world and shot a lion, all in the past six months, and Mr. Lockhart Lampson from the Chamber of Commerce. Also there was old Mrs. Washington Blake, who sponsored Town Hall and, vested in mink, introduced the speakers, and the young Mesdames Cugat, Sturm, and Wagoner, who were being groomed for this.

Close at hand, Mrs. Cugat decided, Captain Derek Allingham appeared, disappointingly, rather more the author than the explorer. He was not quite so winningly boyish as he had appeared on the platform — nor so modest. That engaging trick of debunking his own incredible exploits was apparently just that. Over his shrimp cocktail he seemed, on the whole, rather proud of himself and slightly bored with Town Hall — but very hungry.

'In your travels, Captain, have you, by chance, come upon any fresh physiological criteria of race?' inquired Professor Wiggin, in a measured classroom tone, by way of starting the conversational ball to rolling. Everyone paused, fork raised, politely alert.

'Naturally, Professor,' replied Captain Allingham, swallowing a shrimp and wiping his mouth with deliberation.

'I hope, sir, that you agree with me that the Malay, like the American Indian, merits the status of sub-race, if not of race!' pursued the Professor discursively.

'Unquestionably,' replied the Captain, and scooped up another shrimp.

'Bravo!' exclaimed Professor Wiggin, but this went unacknowledged — leaving the Professor stranded on a somewhat lonely pinnacle of enthusiasm.

Mr. Lockhart Lampson of the Chamber of Com-

merce cleared his throat. 'May I take this opportunity, Captain...' he began carefully, but Miss
Snell of the Book Department slid in ahead: '*I*
would like to inquire,' she said, turning a sudden
pink, 'just how long it takes to pen a masterpiece of
wit and daring such as yours.' Miss Snell employed
for this about the same delicate enunciation that is
required for *the rains in Spain fall mainly in the plains.*

'I write very rapidly,' replied the Captain, cleaning up the last of his cocktail.

'May I take this opportunity...' said Mr. Lockhart Lampson in a firmer tone, but was again
outmaneuvered, this time by young Mr. Porter,
who inquired in man-to-man accents: 'What do you
like for the big cats, Captain, a .470 or a .303?'

'I carry only a .22,' the Captain replied coldly,
poking around among some sweetbreads-under-bell.
Coming upon a piece of ham at the bottom, he
looked pleased.

'May I ——' said Mr. Lampson.

'Dear boy,' said Mrs. Washington Blake, 'all I
could think of during your entire *lecture* was how
your poor mother must have worried!'

'Did you read my book?' asked the Captain
bluntly.

'Well, no — that is, not yet.'

'Mother died when I was born,' he said cheerfully, and retired Mrs. Blake in pitiful disorder.

The Mesdames Cugat, Sturm, and Wagoner had during this rout of the home team remained timidly silent — their only preparation for the encounter having been a light-hearted powdering-up. The rather charming results of this had, however, apparently made some impression. Of his own accord — and with a fair-sized piece of ham still on his plate, too — the Captain turned to Mrs. Sturm, during the pause attendant upon the dissolution of Mrs. Blake, and said, with his famous smile turned on full, 'I say, have you ever had *rijstafel?*'

Mrs. Sturm colored prettily and said, with a slightly British accent, that no, she hadn't.

'You?' he asked, transferring the smile to Mrs. Wagoner.

No, Mrs. Wagoner hadn't either.

Mrs. Cugat, who had decided that *rijstafel* was probably one of those tropical things like beri-beri, was saved just in time by Professor Wiggin, who inquired hesitantly, 'Curry, isn't it?' The Captain gave him a brief nod.

Oh, *curry!* thought Mrs. Cugat happily — she'd had curry. 'Marvelous, isn't it?' she said in reply to the Captain's smile of inquiry.

'Where did you have it?' he demanded eagerly. 'Java, I hope!'

No, Mrs. Cugat said regretfully, not Java — just some people in San Francisco ——

'Unless you've had it at the *Oranje* in Soerabaja,
you don't know what it is,' the Captain declared
flatly. Mrs. Sturm and Mrs. Wagoner looked
pleased.

'I suppose not,' Mrs. Cugat said humbly. 'I've
never been there.' Then she added quite involun-
tarily and unexpectedly, 'My husband has, of
course ——' Mrs. Sturm and Mrs. Wagoner ex-
changed a blank glance.

'Really!' exclaimed the Captain. 'Recently?'

'Well, no,' Mrs. Cugat said, gasping a little in the
bath of her own surprise; 'as a matter of fact — not
since he was little.'

'How did little George like Soerabaja?' asked
Mrs. Sturm acidly.

'He *loved* it,' said Mrs. Cugat, steadying herself.
'He had an old uncle who lived there,' she said in
reasonable explanation to the Captain, and then,
beginning to warm up a little, went on: 'They lived
on a big plantation or something, and George always said it was a perfect circus!'

Captain Allingham looked impressed. 'One of
the big tea-planters, I suppose,' he said enviously.
'They live like kings!'

Mrs. Cugat drew in her horns guiltily. 'Well, I
don't know about *that*,' she said, with a modest
laugh and beset by compunction; 'all I know is, he
was crazy about it!' (Mr. Cugat had a large and

far-flung family — it was conceivable, wasn't it, that one might be a tea-planter?)

'Java!' said the Captain, almost to himself and with a faraway look. 'He's going back, of course, and take *you?*' and somehow he made it sound as if she were the one thing that Java yet lacked.

'I wish he would,' Mrs. Cugat said, dimpling and wondering where Soerabaja was, 'but I'm afraid it's not likely — Uncle Joe died some time ago.'

Old Uncle Joe *Cugat!*' Mrs. Wagoner exclaimed softly, but Mrs. Cugat only nodded in reply, because the Captain had bent toward her again in sympathy. 'How rotten for you!' he said in a low tone, 'but you simply must go back, you know. Let me tell you what happened to me there and you will ——' Then he turned to Mr. Lampson of the Chamber of Commerce in the chair at Mrs. Cugat's side. 'Do give me your seat, will you, old man,' he begged. 'I so seldom find anyone in your country who can bring back Java!'

'May I take this opportunity on behalf. . .' began Mr. Lampson purposefully, but was heartlessly hustled to his feet and into collecting his napkin, silver, water glass, and plate. The rest of the table, smiling in bright envy, began an interchange of polite general conversation, it being evident that what happened to the Captain in Java was to be for Mrs. Cugat's ears alone — the rest of the table, that is, except Mrs. Cugat's two friends Mrs. Sturm and Mrs. Wagoner, who proceeded wordlessly with their lunch, eyes downcast, ears pricked.

The Captain embarked on a colorful tale involving Number One Boys, hill stations, star sapphires, and gin slings. Mrs. Cugat's imagination, always easily incited, flamed in response. Mr. Cugat's childhood with Uncle Joe in Soerabaja became as actual and detailed as yesterday. Salad (Tomato Surprise) and dessert (Bombe Martha) came and went. The rest of the table discussed the Community Chest Drive.

'Will you do one thing for me?' the Captain said at last, over his coffee. 'Will you go back, some day, to the *Concordia* bar and drink a Balaklava Special to me?'

'Of course,' said Mrs. Cugat kindly. 'A Balaklava Special! I've *always* wanted to try one!'

'May I take this opportunity, on behalf of our Junior Members, to welcome you to our midst with the sincere hope that you will find it possible to inspect the work of the Boys' Club?' blurted the now desperate envoy from the Chamber of Commerce.

The Captain looked at Mr. Lampson distantly; then he got out — and glanced into — a little black notebook. 'Ah, yes — the Boys' Club,' he said; 'but I'd like a bit more pudding first.'

'Well, darling, you certainly wowed the Captain,' exclaimed a chorus of admiring voices upon Mrs. Cugat's entrance into the Ladies' Card Room of the Country Club an hour later. 'Where are the two also-rans?'

'I don't know who you mean — aren't they here?' said Mrs. Cugat uncollectedly, adding, with a sheepish grin: 'I had to drop Captain Allingham off at the Boys' Club on my way out. Evie and Sue left me.'

'To go home and clean their guns, I'll bet! You'll pay for this, Mary Elizabeth. How'd you arrange that switch in seats? Everybody in town wants to know.'

'Liz and the Captain had so *much* in common,' said Mrs. Sturm coolly from the doorway. 'It was — uncanny.'

'Well, we *did*,' said Mrs. Cugat guiltily. 'Come on in and cut for deal.'

Mrs. Sturm and Mrs. Wagoner came in and cut composedly, and throughout the afternoon appeared rather noticeably smug, but Mrs. Cugat, still riding the crest, only remarked it casually.

'Isn't it about time for the boys to be out from town?' somebody said eventually, looking out at the dark January dusk.

'They're in the bar now,' said Mrs. Wagoner in a tone of secret satisfaction. 'I heard them come up from the locker room five minutes ago.'

'All right, let's stop. Four rubbers! I could use a cocktail.'

The bar, a pleasant place of paneled oak and bright glass, was filled with men, the espoused, in the main, of Mrs. Cugat's luncheon club. It was maids' night out. Mrs. Cugat entered light-heartedly and with that pleasant little feeling of eagerness commonly attendant upon the seeing of Mr. Cugat again at the end of the day; her eyes combed the crowd. Then they fluttered shut. Mr. Cugat was not there, but at a prominent table with Howie Sturm and Mr. Lampson from the Chamber of Commerce sat Captain Allingham devouring popcorn!

She walked carefully to the far end of the bar and propped herself weakly on it by the elbows, her back to the room. 'Give me a double Scotch,' she whispered.

Evie Sturm's clear voice greeted her husband and his guests. 'Well, you three found each other all right, I see'; and then: 'Where's George Cugat, Howie? I told you to call him for cocktails too.'

Mrs. Cugat took a deep draught of her highball. How did she get herself into things like this? It was incredible! She must be a little crazy — that story of an entirely imaginary Uncle Joe in whatever the name of the place was! Where did it come from? How could she invent a thing like that and actually

almost believe in it? And not be able to stop herself, either! The habit, obviously, was growing —
never before had she been quite so fantastic. It was
horrible, horrible — like kleptomania or something.
And she was caught out for fair this time! Why on
earth couldn't she have said frankly this afternoon,
when they'd asked her: 'Why, of course that was all
a fairy tale, but somebody had to save him, didn't
they? He'd have eaten himself to death.' Something like that. But no, actually her pride in Uncle
Joe hadn't let her. Could George, somehow, be
headed off? He could not. There was his voice on
the stairs now. I'll just stay here in this corner until
it's all over, she thought hopelessly; maybe nobody
will notice me. After that I can slip out and away
and never come back!

'Another double Scotch, Jerry,' she muttered, moving deeper into the shadows, and the bartender looked at her compassionately.

She could not, however, move out of the radius of Mrs. Sturm's voice. 'George, darling!' it said. 'Come and meet Captain Allingham. He wants to hear more about your Uncle Joe from Java!'

Here it comes, thought Mrs. Cugat, hunching her shoulders.

There was a little silence. 'Uncle Joe?' said Mr. Cugat. 'I haven't got any Uncle Joe.'

'No Uncle Joe!' exclaimed Mrs. Sturm delightedly.

'Wha-t!' drawled Mrs. Wagoner.

'You're obviously the wrong Cugat, old man,' said the Captain frigidly. 'The charming little Mrs. Cugat whom I sat next to at lunch had a husband who knew Java well — visited an uncle there as a child — a big tea-planter, she said — some relative, perhaps.'

'It was Liz, all right, George,' put in Mrs. Wagoner's voice with relish. 'I heard her. Old Uncle Joe! Who could she have been talking about?'

'I had an Uncle John in Guam,' said Mr. Cugat reflectively. Mrs. Cugat stiffened. Mr. Cugat laughed suddenly. 'Good Lord!' he said, 'that's who she must have meant — the little idiot; it's the

nearest she ever comes to anything!' Then he turned
to the Captain. 'You know Guam, of course?'

'Oh, rather,' said the Captain. 'Ripping place.'

'Good old Uncle John,' said Mr. Cugat. 'He was
Governor and Big Boy of Guam for years — man in
your position must have met him?'

'Wait, now,' said Captain Allingham. 'What did
you say the name was?'

'Cugat,' said Mr. Cugat. 'John Cugat, U.S.N.,
Retired. He's dead now.'

'Why, of course, old man,' exclaimed the Captain. 'Of course I knew him — how extraordinary!
A wonderful old boy ——'

'Big red beard,' said Mr. Cugat, 'but maybe it
turned white — ?'

'Snow white,' said the Captain. 'Well, well! We
ought to drink to this properly. Can any of these
boys make a Balaklava Special, do you think?'

'A Balaklava Special — !' exclaimed Mr. Cugat.
'There's an idea! Jerry, come here.'

'Hello, darling — hello, Captain,' said Mrs. Cugat,
sauntering up on shaking legs.

Everybody had several Balaklava Specials —
some the Java way, some the Guam way. The
Guam ones had cream in them — Mr. Cugat's
recipe. Captain Allingham, in a discreet under-
tone, told Mr. Cugat about some native customs in
Java; Mr. Cugat told the Captain more about Uncle

John in Guam; they clapped each other on the back.

'Did you drink many of these as a child, George?' Mrs. Sturm asked curiously, over her third.

'Hardly,' Mr. Cugat laughed, 'but our Number Five Boy came to this country and he taught my father how to make them.'

'How'd the boy work out over here?' inquired the Captain.

'Badly,' said Mr. Cugat. 'He married an Irish girl and went all to pieces!'

Mrs. Cugat sat very quietly in spite of two double Scotches and a Balaklava Special; she was giving thanks — to Providence, to Mr. Cugat, to Uncle John of Guam, to God. 'I'm never going to whiffle again,' she said humbly to herself, '*ever!*'

The next night Anna set before Mr. Cugat his favorite dessert — Floating Island. 'Well, well — as I live,' he said facetiously, 'another Balaklava Special!'

'George,' Mrs. Cugat said quietly, 'I went to see your Aunt Edith today.'

Mr. Cugat dipped out an island with care.

'She says that your Uncle John has lived in Kennebunkport, Maine, for the last forty years and never was in Guam in his life.'

'This enough for you?' said Mr. Cugat, without meeting her eye.

'George! Look at me —— Were *you* whiffling last night?'

Mr. Cugat reddened, then he said brusquely: 'Well, hell, darling, I couldn't leave you stuck with that terrible Java story, could I? Your little pals were getting ready to throw you to the lions ——'

'But George,' she exclaimed, awed, 'you were perfectly wonderful! Do you mean to say that — Guam — and all that cream — and the Number Five Boy and the Irish girl were —*your own?*'

'Wasn't bad, was it?' Mr. Cugat said modestly.

Mrs. Cugat continued to look at him blankly; then she said, 'But I don't understand ——'

'What?'

'Captain Allingham said he knew Uncle John — he said he knew him well — he said his beard was snow white ——'

Mr. Cugat's lip curled. 'Your wonderful Captain Allingham,' he said disgustedly, 'is nothing but a damned liar.'

...*just cause*...

'Did Cory get home today as planned?' asked Mrs. Cugat, as she and Mr. Cugat sat down to dinner one early spring evening.

'My, yes,' replied Mr. Cugat in the fond, indulgent tone which any reference to this Damon to his Pythias invariably provoked. 'And is he full of himself! If the trip did old lady Bonbright half the good it did him — she's good for another twenty years.'

'Well, I'm glad he got something out of it,' Mrs. Cugat said tenderly. 'Not many men, who like a good time as much as he does, would be willing to spend a whole month taking a cruise with a sick old aunt — particularly a poor aunt. It was the sweetest thing I ever heard of! Did he have *any* fun at all?'

'I don't know — he's brown as a berry and beaming all over.' Then he added thoughtfully, 'He's

coming over after dinner — he says he's got something to tell us.'

'Something to *tell* us?'

'Yes,' said Mr. Cugat uneasily. 'You don't suppose, do you —?'

'Good Heavens — of course! He's got himself
engaged again!'

'He shows all the regular symptoms,' admitted
Mr. Cugat somberly.

Cory, arriving immediately at the conclusion of
dinner, came in almost bashfully. He showed all
the regular symptoms, Mrs. Cugat thought wryly,
and then a few. He positively shone, and had a
smily, secret look that could have been spotted
across the street.

'Darling, how well you look!' she exclaimed,
kissing him warmly. 'Sit down and tell us everything — we want to hear it all.'

'Well,' said Mr. Cartwright, clearing his throat
and beginning to tack nervously back and forth
across the room with his hands in his pockets, 'it
was pretty swell.'

'What's she look like?' offered Mrs. Cugat helpfully.

He turned a deep garnet and grinned gratefully.
'Like a goddess,' he said huskily.

'Not old Liberty?' flippantly interposed Mr.
Cugat to cover his anxiety. 'Myself, I think the
type a little heavy ——'

'No, seriously, you two,' said Cory, 'this is the *real* thing at last. I want you to be the first to know. Look!' And with trembling fingers he produced a white velvet, gold-tooled box from his coat pocket, which he opened to display a really superb ruby.

'Why, Cory, it's lovely!' breathed Mrs. Cugat in actual awe. 'What a lucky girl she is! Now stop fooling and answer a few questions.' But she could not begin her catechism, of course, until Mr. Cugat had got through devoutly voiced congratulations; they had each taken a good poke at the other to clear the air, and then Mr. Cugat exclaimed, 'How about a drink to the bride!' This had all happened once or twice before, so she waited patiently.

'Now, then, tell me!' she demanded, as Mr. Cugat hastened to the pantry.

'Well, her name's Claiborne Calhoun and I met her on the boat and she's a blonde and from Virginia and she was taking the cruise to get over a fall she had off a horse,' replied Cory, making an obvious effort to stick to bare informative facts and not panegyrize any more than he could help. 'She looks sort of like you, Liz — aristocratic-like — only she's taller and more wholesome-looking — I mean, you know — a little more the athletic type.'

'Why, darling, she sounds lovely!' Mrs. Cugat exclaimed generously; 'just the kind I'd always hoped you'd find. Did you meet the family?'

'No, she had only "Birdie" along to look after her — "Birdie's" sort of an ex-governess. But I'm going down there this week-end —— It's marvelous at this time of year and we're going to announce it on a hunt or something. Claiborne's joint master of the Old Commonwealth.'

They proceeded to drink toasts: to the bride and to the Old Commonwealth and to the S.S. *American Manufacturer* and to Cape Hatteras — off which, in a severe blow, realization of Cory's worth had come to Claiborne — and to 'Birdie' and to old lady Bonbright, who, fortuitously, had remained bedded with lumbago from the second day out.

'Well,' said Mrs. Cugat, as they finally closed the front door on Cory's by then, dreamy countenance, 'I really believe she's very suitable.'

'She sounds all right, at that,' acknowledged Mr. Cugat. Then he added anxiously, 'I hope you two get on.'

'Oh, we will,' Mrs. Cugat yawned, 'don't worry about that. I'd do anything to see Cory settled down and happy with the right girl, and this time I have a feeling everything's going to turn out well.' Mr. Cugat kissed her tenderly and they climbed the stairs, rather spent.

A week later they got a midnight telegram. 'Announcing it Saturday. Need you. Cory,' it said tersely. Mr. Cugat, huddled in his bathrobe, read it frowning and rubbed his chin.

'He sounds sort of desperate,' Mrs. Cugat commented, peering out anxiously from under her quilt. 'Do you suppose everything's all right?'

'I don't know. Would you like to go? We could drive down for the week-end. It might be a pretty nice trip.'

'Oh I'd love it!' she cried. 'What fun!' and dove beneath the quilt again to begin planning her clothes.

It *was* a nice trip. They left on Thursday — unprecedented for Mr. Cugat, who was wont to say that *his* week-ends began Saturday noon — stayed the night at a country hotel and drove leisurely on the next morning over clear sunny roads through snow-patched mountains.

'What a lovely part of the country to live in,' murmured Mrs. Cugat, smiling in pleasure as they passed a rolling field dappled with horses, a sun-splashed ravine, and a tiny brass-knockered house behind an old stone wall. 'Maybe, since Claiborne likes to hunt, Cory will have a place down here and we can come to visit often.'

'Maybe,' said Mr. Cugat, committing himself to nothing yet. 'You know, we ought to be almost there — the Calhoun place should be just east of that last town we came through. We'd better stop and ask.'

'All right,' she said, 'the next man we see ——'

and then: 'Oh darling, be careful! Those sweet dogs ——' They had rounded a turn in the narrow road and come abruptly upon a small meandering pack of hounds in the charge of a shambling individual in a long white coat. He carried a hunting-whip which he was flicking with all the unconcern possible, but, as the lash seemed possessed to wrap itself around his neck, the effect lacked nonchalance. Hearing the Cugats' car, he tucked the whip hastily underneath his arm and shooed the pack off the road with the long skirts of the coat — like **an old** woman shooing chickens with her apron.

'Can you tell us the way to the Calhoun place?' called Mr. Cugat, drawing to a stop, and the figure turned. '*Cory*, you old son-of-a-gun!'

It was, in truth, Mr. Cartwright, but Mrs. Cugat was shocked at the change in him. His face looked

drawn and actually surly. This expression, however, as he looked up was washed away almost immediately by one of clear and touching joy.

'He*llo!*' he yelped, dropping the whip at the bottom of the ditch and scrambling up the bank to the
car. 'I'd hardly dared hope for you before dinner-
time!'

'There go your dogs!' exclaimed Mr. Cugat,
pointing to a mass of wriggling sterns disappearing
over a wall.

'Let 'em go; they know their way home better
than I do, anyway. Move over, let me in ——
Gosh, but it's good to see you two!'

'Where's Claiborne?' queried Mrs. Cugat, 'and
what are you doing mooching along 'way out here
with all those dogs?'

'Hounds, pet, call them hounds. *Never* dogs.
These are the lady hounds, and all about to become mothers. I have to take them for a damned
walk every morning!' Then he added shortly,
'Claiborne's at the kennels.'

He settled down between them and, lighting a
cigarette, relaxed gratefully. 'Turn to the left at
the next crossroads,' he said; 'and don't hurry.'

They drove along, happy together in the sharp,
misty morning, but Cory seemed to have very little
to say. Pretty soon they turned through wide gates
and wound between rail fences. A fat white horse

rolled and kicked in the sun; a brown mare with her leggy black baby trotted over to watch them pass; Mrs. Cugat was enchanted.

'Oh, Cory,' she exclaimed, 'what a perfectly beautiful place! Don't you love it? When I think of the country around home! Nothing but tractors, signboards, barbed wire, hot-dog stands ——'

'Uh-huh,' said Cory.

The house, when they reached it, sent Mrs. Cugat into further transports. Its porches were traditionally pillared, and vine-fringed balconies hung from upper windows; the door stood hospitably open to reveal delicate soaring stairs and a bright fire; an old colored man in a plum-colored coat with flat silver buttons hobbled down to open the luggage compartment.

'Make yourselves at home,' said Cory when they'd reached their charming beruffled bedroom. 'I'm going to take a bath and get this stink off.'

'What's the matter with him?' asked Mrs. Cugat when the door had closed. 'He seems sort of grouchy.'

'I don't know,' said Mr. Cugat slowly.

Miss Claiborne Calhoun looked exactly like a goddess — one of those blonde north-country ones. She came striding up from the direction of the kennels, expertly cracking her hunting-whip, just as Mr. and Mrs. Cugat emerged onto the porch after unpacking and changing into their best country clothes. Not once did the lash wind round her neck. She was dressed in breeches and canvas leggins and had on a filthy long white coat like Cory's, but Mrs. Cugat could notice nothing but her head, which was small and gilt and superbly set on her boyishly broad shoulders. Her eyes were the color of larkspur and had a level look, and her brown forehead was not femininely rounded but in beautifully modeled planes like a man's. She looked very wholesome. She made Mrs. Cugat, in spite of her new tweed suit, feel like a nasty, curvesome little Dresden shepherdess.

'Welcome to Green Trees,' she said in a clear light voice and a buttoned-up British accent. 'Have you managed to make yourselves comfortable?' She gripped their hands with cool, strong fingers and then called through the front door: 'Enos! Enos! Where's Mr. Clay?'

'Yes'm, Miz Claiborne. Mist' Clay, he's out in the dinin'-room fixin' a toddy,' gobbled the old negro with the plum coat, hastening into view. 'Mistuh Cartwright, tho', he just took himself a stiff peg and went right back up to his room ag'in.'

Miss Calhoun laughed lightly. 'Take a toddy up to him, Enos,' she said amusedly; 'he doesn't think he wants lunch.' At that moment a long-nosed young man in a sagging and sun-faded tweed coat

and worn breeches and boots emerged from the
dining-room carrying five toddies on a tray. 'The
Cugats, Clay. This is Clay Lowrie, the better half
of the Old Commonwealth.'

Mr. Lowrie acknowledged the introductions and
put the tray down. 'What was the matter with
Cartwright, Cal?' he asked curiously. 'He looked
like he was goin' to be sick.'

'He *was* sick,' she replied, with a little underlying
scorn in her tone, 'on the pumphouse floor.' Then
she went on, laughing: 'Melody whelped last night
— ten — and all rather small — and Cory and I
had just looked them over and gone out on the stoop
to sit in the sun when out came Leighton after us
with the runt and two others he didn't want and
snapped their heads against a wheelbarrow. Poor
Cory; after all, he *had* only just left off mooing and
poking at the runt because he thought it showed
personality or something. Leighton ought, really,
be a little more considerate of guests, I think.'

Mr. Lowrie smiled thinly. 'Cartwright will have
to get used to our li'l' ways,' he said.

Mrs. Cugat drank deeply of her toddy.

'I think I'll go take a look at him,' said Mr. Cugat,
getting up abruptly.

Cory appeared for lunch, looking pale, but
dressed in extremely beautiful and very new riding-
clothes. 'Your boot garters are on backwards, my

love,' Miss Calhoun remarked, giving him a cool glance over her soup. Then she went on to explain to Mrs. Cugat about her mother and father. They lived in Washington, she said, when they weren't in London, but, as for her, she couldn't swallow New Deal Washington. She and 'Birdie,' when they weren't in London, lived here at Green Trees. 'Birdie's somewhere about,' Miss Calhoun said carelessly. 'Probably fussing over the announcement party tonight. I left it all to her — I can't think of anything but My Lady Satin. Clay, I've decided to breed her!'

'Well! You came to it at last, eh? That mare's been navicular for six months, but you just wouldn't admit she was through.'

'I know — I couldn't bear to — my own lovely Satin ——' Miss Calhoun's clear, crisp voice had taken on an entirely new note — roughened and warm.

'What are you sendin' her to?' Mr. Lowrie inquired interestedly.

'Well,' she hesitated, 'Randolph's got Chance Gallant still standing at Foxes' Hole ——'

Mr. Lowrie hooted. 'Chance Gallant! My Lord, baby, you haven't a hope!'

'Oh, I knew you'd laugh,' she said wistfully. 'Leighton did too — but I've got my heart set on him — *nothing's* too good for my Satin.'

'Chance Gallant is, honey,' he said gently. 'In the first place, the fee is 'way over your head; in the second place, his book is full until year after next; and in the third place, "No maidens need apply."' Miss Calhoun looked disconsolate. Then he added, 'Besides, he isn't still standin' at Foxes' Hole — they shipped to Kentucky yesterday.'

'Oh, they did!' Her voice sounded small and squeezed now, but she lifted her proud little head gamely. 'Well, I guess that's that. I kept hoping like a fool that as long as he was still in the neighborhood I might work it somehow.'

'Plenty of good stallions around within reason,' comforted Mr. Lowrie. 'Take my Null and Void, for instance ——'

Mr. and Mrs. Cugat nodded and smiled and clucked in polite sympathy throughout this, but Cory, usually the most responsive of guests, ate on stolidly.

'Now we'll *all* go out and look at the horses,' he said suddenly as they finally pushed back their chairs.

'That's right, darling,' said Miss Calhoun in a surprised voice. 'I was just going to suggest it!' and she gave him the first nice look that the Cugats had seen sent in his direction all day. Its effect was pathetic — he bounded to meet it like an ecstatic spaniel. If Miss Calhoun had said, 'Down, Cory-boy, *down*, I say!' Mrs. Cugat would not have been in the least surprised.

The stables were extensive. Mrs. Cugat was impressed. They idled along past box after box, stopping a little before each one to discuss and pat its occupant. A bowlegged, monosyllabic man in high-waisted breeches accompanied them, as well as the murderer, Leighton. Miss Calhoun and Mr. Lowrie made assertions and disagreed and disputed aimably at every stall; Leighton diplomatically siding first with one and then with the other. The high-waisted man spat philosophically and opened and closed doors and produced sugar. The horses leaned out sociably. Mrs. Cugat wondered how, with so many horses, they ever remembered which was which, and halfway through stopped paying much attention and simply gave herself up to enjoying her surroundings. The stable was very pleasant — it had a nice smell — not ammoniac like the livery stable at home, but clean and pungent and leathery. The stalls had beautifully stained doors with wrought-iron hinges and brass nameplates (that's how they told!), and in the tack room hung row upon row of shining saddles and ribbony bridles.

Mr. Cugat asked intelligent questions and appeared vastly interested — she was proud of him — but Cory lounged along looking half asleep and ventured little. Once he did timidly tweak a curl behind his beloved's ear, when he apparently thought Mr. Lowrie wasn't looking, but Miss Calhoun was at the time asserting witheringly that, as everybody knew, some old crock of Mr. Lowrie's had been gone in the wind for a year and he was a perfect ass to hold out for two hundred. She, though, might give him one-seventy-five, she let fall craftily — and brushed at the curl with impatience.

In the last and largest box with the biggest and shiniest nameplate lived My Lady Satin. 'Lovely-Lovely,' crooned Miss Calhoun, stepping into the stall and rubbing her clear brown cheek against the shining neck. My Lady Satin pawed the floor and bunted Miss Calhoun around affectionately. Cory looked out the window. 'Come, darling, and show the lady and gentleman what a Beautiful you are! Come on, girl — come, Gorgeous.' My Lady Satin tossed her head and rolled her eyes, but was finally prevailed upon to put her head in a halter and emerge. She looked just like any other horse to Mrs. Cugat, only bigger and nearer. Mrs. Cugat grasped Mr. Cugat's arm and held on tight, and My Lady Satin swished her tail and whinnied.

'Did you ever,' asked Miss Calhoun of Mr. Cugat, with a misty, love-clouded look, 'see anything more perfect than this?'

'She's a beauty, all right!' said Mr. Cugat en-
thusiastically, and ran a professional-looking eye
over My Lady Satin and stroked her neck fearlessly.
Mrs. Cugat watched him in admiration; then, for
some reason, she looked at Mr. Lowrie — he was
watching Miss Calhoun, and with a surprising expression on his sharp face. He looked tender. Cory
continued to gaze dully out the window.

However, this rapt though disparate atmosphere
was suddenly shattered; from outside came rapidly
approaching sounds of tumult. My Lady Satin
was turned over to the high-waisted man summarily
and they all rushed to the door. The stable yard
was full of hounds and, bounding up the path from
the gate, came an apoplectic young man in a cover-
all, whipping and slashing the rear rank mercilessly
and blistering the air with oaths. A few of the
hounds were coupled together, but on most the
couples dangled broken. Some still held on to what
may, at one time, have been a white chicken, and
all were splashed with blood. One proudly lugged
along a large gray gander — very dead.

'Why, Patton, what is it? Clay, *look!* They're
the bitches in whelp!' exclaimed Miss Calhoun.
Then she turned to Cory: 'How did this happen?
What have you done? Didn't you put them *in*
when you brought them back this morning?'

'Lord,' said Cory, 'that's right. They beat it

off over a stone wall when Liz and George drove along, but I was so tickled I just let 'em go. I figured they'd get home all right, knowing the country so well. Of course I meant to tell you, but, with one thing and another, I forgot.'

'They done a good two hundred dollars' worth of damage to me,' snarled the man named Patton. 'Rioted all over my young box, killed a dozen or more hens, two shoats, and that gander.'

Mr. Lowrie and Leighton took immediate and admirable charge.

'Wait here, Patton,' said Miss Calhoun curtly, 'while I go down to the kennels with them and see how many are missing.'

Mr. and Mrs. Cugat and Cory waited with Mr.

Patton and heard again, and with embellishment, this frightful tale of pillage. Mr. Cugat looked grave, and Cory stricken. Mrs. Cugat patted Cory's hand comfortingly, but could think of nothing much to say.

'Mr. Lowrie will see you the first thing in the morning, Patton,' Miss Calhoun said, coming back up the path with Leighton. 'Figure it all up and we'll make it right. We're both very sorry. Such things don't happen often with this pack, you know.'

Mr. Patton departed, looking vindictive.

'God, Leighton, it would be Patton, wouldn't it!' exclaimed Miss Calhoun, slapping agitatedly at her boot with her crop. 'Now he'll probably take down our post and rail, and put up an electric fence or something. He's one of those progressive farmer boys,' she explained to Mr. Cugat, 'who went to agricultural school in Nebraska or somewhere — we've been handling him with kid gloves. Now this!' She turned on her heel and stalked into the house. Not once had she directed her ire at, or even looked upon, Cory. Mrs. Cugat watched her retreating figure in some admiration.

She appeared again almost immediately, however, well in hand, and proceeded to arrange the afternoon for the pleasure of her guests. She and Cory and Mr. Cugat could exercise some horses, she said; Mr. Lowrie, in the car, could go and look at fences

with **Mrs.** Cugat, who — wasn't she correct —
hadn't sat on a horse for some time? She was correct.
Mrs. Cugat hadn't sat on anything even resembling
a horse since she'd been led around the park on a
Shetland pony, screaming, at the age of six. Mrs.
Cugat didn't think looking at fences (of all things)
with the sardonic Mr. Lowrie sounded much fun,
but she was politely anxious to fall in with any plans.

They were, however, some time getting started
because of Mr. Cugat's calves. Not booted since
he was a polo-playing stripling, they had apparently
muscled up and his boots wouldn't go on. A pair
of Mr. Lowrie's were tried and a pair of Leighton's,
and then a pair produced by Miss Calhoun which
belonged to her father. These, at last, he managed
to squeeze into.

'They're rather nice ones,' Miss Calhoun commented. 'Pa won them in a crap game off the Duke
of Windsor.'

There was more to looking at fences with Mr.
Lowrie than Mrs. Cugat had expected. True, they
bumped up one lane and down another and Mr.
Lowrie scanned fences on both sides with a sharp
eye while she drove; sometimes even getting out to
shake a post or rattle a bar or stamp on the ground
in front of a fence; but they also paid a lot of calls.
As soon as they'd come to a farmhouse, however
small, he'd tell her to turn in. The dour Mr. Lowrie,

paying calls on farmers, waxed almost genial. Mrs. Cugat was surprised — he seemed very popular. He'd ask about new babies, chronic ailments, and the state of crops; graciously sample drinks, pipe tobacco, and baked goods, and always, and without fail, look at a horse.

This last was hard on Mrs. Cugat, who had to get quite close to a number of horses with no Mr. Cugat there to cling to. But she covered her terror as best she could.

'Are you trying to buy a horse?' she asked curiously, after a particularly long and footling discussion as to the merits of a shaggy flea-bitten gray, which had been proudly led out and trotted around a barnyard.

'No, they're tryin' to sell me a horse,' Mr. Lowrie replied — almost happily.

'Why are they trying to sell you a horse?' she queried.

'There's not a person in Virginia won't try to sell you a horse,' he said. 'It's in 'em.'

'Why do we keep looking at their horses, then?' asked Mrs. Cugat, determined to get to the bottom of this.

'My dear young lady, I'm a master of hounds,' he replied with dignity. 'And,' he went on, 'I flatter myself — rather a good one. That is, in so far as lookin' after the country and keepin' in with the

farmers goes. We ride over some of their land, you
see. It takes a lot of time, but it's my job and I like
it — and them.'

Mrs. Cugat subsided, somewhat squelched. 'Besides,' he added, 'I just might run into a bargain.'

'There's Foxes' Hole,' he said a few minutes later,
pointing with his ever-in-hand hunting-whip to an
imposing white house with innumerable green-
roofed out-buildings and sweeping gravelled drives.
'That's the Randolph place. Randolph's the owner
of Chance Gallant, you know.' Then, as Mrs.
Cugat looked unimpressed, 'The stallion Cal was
talkin' about at lunch. He *is* a horse, I will say, and
between you and me is bringin' a higher stud fee
now than Man O' War in his best days. Cal's had
her heart set on a Chance Gallant foal out of Satin
ever since the mare went lame, but of course she'd be
a fool to risk the price even if they'd consent to
take her. Satin's a beauty, but hardly in that class.
Cal, though, is crazier about that mare than anything — or anybody — in the world. It's too bad
the stallion's gone — I'd take you in to see him.'

They drove on, Mrs. Cugat giving silent thanks
that there was one less horse in Virginia to look at,
especially one less stallion — the word sounded
fire-breathing.

'One more stop, straight down this road and then
home,' said Mr. Lowrie. 'This won't take long, it's

just old Lecorn — I want to speak to him about haulin' some rails for me.'

Old Lecorn was almost the unpleasantest-looking man she had ever seen. One side of his face was sort of hooked up, which stretched the eye shut; besides which he seemed slightly half-witted. Terms were discussed over the front gate anent the hauling of a load of rails by Lecorn's team of mules, and then, as usual, they repaired to the barn.

'That's a cute horse,' said Mrs. Cugat, still politely determined to keep up her end.

'That's a jackass, mam,' said Lecorn with a crooked, squinting smile.

'Oh, it *is!*' exclaimed Mrs. Cugat. 'Well! What do you do with jackasses, now?'

'Jackass on a mare gets a mule,' Mr. Lowrie put in briefly.

'Oh, I see! Oh.' Would she, Mrs. Cugat wondered, after a little more time in Virginia —?

They arrived home to find Mr. Cugat prostrate and pale in a porch chair, several people working over him anxiously. The Duke of Windsor's boots would not come off.

'A li'l' tight, eh?' said Mr. Lowrie, sauntering up the steps.

'What do *you* think!' barked Cory, tenderly holding a brimming straightshot to Mr. Cugat's lips.

'Ah knowed a man once't who hadda have both laigs sawed off,' old Enos reminisced. 'His boots stuck tight an' the blud all stopped an' his laigs jus' died.'

'I'm really afraid they'll have to be cut, Clay,' Miss Calhoun said sadly, and Mrs. Cugat paled. 'The boots, I mean,' she added patiently. 'We've worked and worked, but his legs have swollen now, and you know how that feels. He's about all in.'

Mr. Lowrie gave her a long sympathetic look and then set to work with his knife. The Duke of Windsor's boots, evidently considered rather in the light of a museum piece, were not cut without a pang. Mr. Cugat, finally released, was helped wobbling up the stairs. It was time to dress for the announcement party.

The party was lovely. 'Birdie' (a Miss Byrd, lacking none of the Admiral's talents for accomplishment) must have felt amply repaid by the results of her 'fussing.' The drawing-room was candlelit, the stairway hung with green; beaming negroes ladled champagne cup from burnished bowls, and the guests looked beautiful and distinguished. Women wore their grandmothers' jewelry — men, pink evening coats. Mr. Cugat and Cory, honest in tuxedos, looked a little like somebody got in to keep an eye on the flat silver.

Intuition, however, had told Mrs. Cugat to bring her off-the-shoulder black lace, and she looked lovely. So, in white tulle, did Miss Calhoun. Miss Calhoun looked radiant. There were only a chosen few, however, who knew that this radiance was not altogether induced by joy in her own betrothal — Mr. Randolph of Foxes' Hole was among those present! And it was not to be bruited about, but he was *not* sending Chance Gallant to Kentucky until *next* week! Furthermore, by way of an engagement present to the daughter of his oldest friend, he had expansively promised that Chance Gallant would be at home to My Lady Satin at *any* time and on a purely social footing. (For an *engagement* present! thought Mr. and Mrs. Cugat, strangers in a strange land.) Mr. Lowrie congratulated Miss Calhoun on her extraordinary good luck. Cory remained apathetic.

The party waxed gayer and gayer and the drawing-room floor was cleared for dancing. Mrs. Cugat
found herself in great demand, and Mr. Cugat,
gradually regaining the use of his legs, trod a careful
measure. Virginians were nice, they confided to
each other, if caught singly. Two Virginians, of
course, talked horse.

At the height of the gaiety, however, the little
high-waisted man from the stables appeared in the
door, beckoning urgently. 'Miss Claiborne, Miss
Claiborne,' he whispered, 'you'd better come.
Merry Margaret looks like foalin'.'

'Right away, Reagan,' she said quickly and, without hesitation, left the arms of a pink-coated gallant
who waltzed like a dream and slipped briskly into
the dirty white coat held for her.

'Don't you want me to come with you?' offered
Mr. Lowrie.

'No,' she replied lightly. 'Cory will. It will be
tremendously interesting for him — believe it or
not, he's never seen a foal born! Carry on here,
Clay, as host. You know Merry Margaret — it
may be hours.' Cory gave Mr. Lowrie a triumphant
look and with a springy step followed his betrothed
out into the night.

It was early in the following rosy dawn that
Mrs. Cugat woke suddenly to hear him come in.
She sat up in bed and listened. He was being sick
in the bathroom.

'Darling, what do you really think about this engagement?' Mrs. Cugat whispered worriedly, as she and Mr. Cugat dressed next morning.

'He's done it this time,' Mr. Cugat said, leaning over with a groan to tie his shoe.

'George, he doesn't fit in down here and he never will,' persisted Mrs. Cugat. 'I want to cry every time I look at him — cute, funny Cory, who's never at a loss and the life of every party —— Why, he's miserable! He can have pretty near any girl in the world he wants and goes and picks one like Claiborne. I can't imagine what she'll do at home — none of us ever breed anything!'

'I know,' said Mr. Cugat slowly. 'That's the trouble with a shipboard romance — everybody's out of his true environment and bathed in tropical moonlight —— The trouble is now that Claiborne and Cory are both too gentlemanly to break it up.'

'Well, I'm not,' said Mrs. Cugat, fluffing out her hair spiritedly. 'I never did like fine gentlemanly women, anyway!'

'Now, Liz,' warned Mr. Cugat anxiously, 'remember it's none of your business.'

'None of my business! If that's not just like a man — you feel much worse about it than I do, but you'd just sit by and watch him ruin his life and not raise a finger!'

'There's nothing in the world I wouldn't do for

Cory,' declaimed Mr. Cugat heatedly, 'but some things are taboo. Women don't understand.'

'I'll say they don't!' retorted Mrs. Cugat in scorn, and they descended to the dining-room.

A number of people were there — everyone dressed in hunting-clothes. Claiborne looked like a slim young English prince. Mr. Lowrie, Mrs. Cugat thought, was the only man she had ever seen on whom a pink coat did not look like fancy dress. It looked as if it grew on him. Poor Cory, though, evidently at the mercy of some cruel custom which Mrs. Cugat decided was probably designed to put probationary hunters at the biggest disadvantage possible, was unbecomingly garbed in a senatorial-looking black coat, a wispy white stock, and a somewhat low derby, locked on with a cord. He looked like a lugubrious monkey on a stick.

'Tie his stock for him, will you, Clay?' Miss Calhoun begged in passing. 'He's got it right over left again.'

Mrs. Cugat simmered.

Mr. and Mrs. Cugat watched the hunt from a car. What they could see of it. And what they could see of it, Mrs. Cugat didn't think much of — little mechanical-looking figures moving across a hillside or standing interminably about against a dark mass of trees. Only once did Mr. Cugat exclaim, 'By George, there he goes! Close along that fence!' and train his glasses on a near-by hill.

Mrs. Cugat bounced with excitement. 'He's winning, he's winning!' she cried as the field thundered by and sailed a stone wall, Cory back in his saddle and well in the lead of everybody, including hounds.

They drove back to Green Trees after a time and ate luncheon alone with 'Birdie.' There was no tellin' when the hunters would come in, she said. She herself was goin' to take a nap. Mr. Cugat thought this an excellent idea and repaired to his room. Mrs. Cugat wandered into the drawing-room and sank into a high-backed chair with a copy of *Blood Horse*, which she thought might prove instructive. It didn't, for she dozed off, and only woke with a start to find it dusk and herself an embarrassed eavesdropper.

'Cal, honey, are you still goin' through with this ridiculous engagement business?' asked Mr. Lowrie's drawling voice behind her with an almost appealing note of pleading.

'Certainly,' came Miss Calhoun's clipped accents; 'and why not, may I ask?' She was apparently slapping at her boot with her whip again.

'Why not, Cal! You ask that! You must have had your eyes shut all day.'

'Yes?'

'Yes, you know what I'm talkin' about. Your hero not only kept well out in front of the huntsman all the time, but he trampled Bugler, Dido, and Merrylegs in a lane, galloped over Patton's crocus bed and cut in on Mrs. Fairchild at a five-barred gate that she was goin' at like a train. He refused the gate, of course.'

'He couldn't hold his horse,' said Miss Calhoun shortly.

'Exactly,' said Mr. Lowrie; 'and what was his horse? None other than old Snowball, who carried your eight-year-old cousin all last season without a mistake. I did what I could for him.'

'Oh, you know Snowball, Clay. She's got a mouth of iron if you take hold of it.'

'Well, that lad takes a nice hold, all right. To think of a *Calhoun* marryin' a man with bad hands!'

Miss Calhoun said nothing.

'Furthermore,' said Mr. Lowrie disgustedly, 'he'd get lonesome or somethin' and ride up to pass the time o' day every time hounds were findin' — but to top all, after the kill he went behind a tree and was sick.'

'Not again!' she sighed.

'Oh, Cal, look at this thing sensibly. They're nice enough fellows, both of them — a couple of weanlin' financiers. But what do *you* want with a man like that? You won't even need his fortune after he's made it. And what are you goin' to do for huntin'? Cugat says in their country they hunt wolves —

from Lincoln Zephyrs — with automatic shot-guns!'

Mrs. Cugat's eyes widened — Mr. Cugat's ways were devious!

'Oh shut up!' Miss Calhoun's voice sounded strained.

'That's right, take it out on me. You've got the worst temper of any woman I ever saw and you haven't let fly at him once, although he's done enough to drive you off your head.'

'I know, Clay,' she said huskily, 'but you don't understand. You just can't get mad at him. He's one of those people that nobody's ever been mad at, I believe. He's really a darling — but not himself down here, somehow. On the boat he was wonderful.'

'Maybe I'm wonderful on a boat too; you've never seen me.' Mr. Lowrie's voice was getting husky too. Mrs. Cugat hunched in her chair uncomfortably.

'I've seen you on a horse, dear,' Miss Calhoun said gently. 'You don't have to show me how wonderful you are.'

'I'd like to try showin' you on a boat,' Mr. Lowrie said wistfully, and Mrs. Cugat's heart went suddenly out to him. Poor Mr. Lowrie, only known to be wonderful on a horse — he'd never get anywhere. Whereas Cory —— But there were Claiborne and

Cory — both gentlemen and helpless. Claiborne herself had admitted — almost tearfully — that nobody could get mad at Cory. If only someone could just make her get mad at him! Mrs. Cugat, who was no gentleman, huddled thoughtfully down in her chair.

'Shall we go look at the horses?' said Miss Calhoun brightly as they arose that evening from an early supper.

'I saw the horses yesterday,' said Mr. Cugat innocently, and sauntered out into the hall to look for the New York papers.

'So did I,' muttered Cory, hobbling painfully after him, 'but haven't you found out yet that in Virginia we look at the damned horses after every damned meal!'

Miss Calhoun blinked — surprised and hurt. 'Darling, I didn't know you felt that way about it,' she remonstrated. 'Of course we do! My poor Lady Satin! She'd be heart-broken if I didn't come to see her.'

'Lady Satin, faugh!' exploded Cory in magnificent contempt. 'I wish that big Spark Plug'd never been born!'

'Why, Cory,' said Mrs. Cugat, in an anxious endeavor to dispel tension. 'I believe you're jealous.'

'That's me, all right,' he snorted. 'Jealous of a

three-legged horse!' and limped sputtering out of sight.

'I'll go with you, Claiborne,' Mrs. Cugat said valiantly. 'I love looking at those beautiful horses.'

Fortunately for her, Leighton was waiting in the yard. 'Miss Claiborne,' he said, 'I made a mistake about that Upperville sale; it's Monday instead of Tuesday. We'll have to go over tomorrow.'

'That's bad — I'll have to leave a houseful of guests ——'

'Please don't worry about us, Claiborne,' protested Mrs. Cugat. 'We'll get along all right. If it's something important ——'

'It is,' Miss Calhoun said thoughtfully. 'There's a chance to pick up something pretty good in brood mares at that sale. Lord! and I wanted to send Satin to Foxes' Hole tomorrow too, before Randolph changes his mind. But if you and I and Ned go with the van, Leighton, that leaves nobody on the place but the kennel boy or Reagan to drive her over in the trailer, and I don't trust either one of them with it on these hills. I have it, though!' — she turned to Mrs. Cugat — 'Cory's good with cars. Why can't Reagan load her and then George and Cory run her down — if they will? I could phone Foxes' Hole tonight that she's coming, and then all they'll have to do is wait while she's unloaded and drive the trailer back.'

Mr. Cugat and Cory appeared, strolling together through the dusk, and the subject was tactfully broached. Both said sure and that they'd drive *very* carefully.

'How far is it — dear?' asked Cory, sounding timid.

'Just up the road,' said Leighton, 'you can't miss it. Big trees, white gate, green mailbox, and they'll be expecting you.'

Mr. Cugat and Cory lit their pipes and strolled away — in the opposite direction, however, from the stables.

'May I borrow the station wagon?' asked Mrs. Cugat suddenly. 'I want to send a telegram.'

'Phone it,' said Miss Calhoun.

'I'll go, I believe — there's something I want to get. The stores are open on Saturday night, aren't they?' She was halfway to the garage.

'What in time are you doing?' Mr. Cugat muttered, sticking his head out of the covers at five o'clock the next morning.

'Shhh!' whispered Mrs. Cugat. 'I woke up, so I just thought I'd go out and help poor Cory with those hounds. I don't want him to get in any worse than he is! You go back to sleep.'

'I certainly will!' sputtered Mr. Cugat. '*Hounds!*'

Mrs. Cugat slipped back into the bedroom several hours later, disheveled and weary. Mr. Cugat was not there. She could hear him and Cory and Reagan out in the yard loading My Lady Satin into the trailer. Miss Calhoun, Leighton, and Ned had left at daybreak, as planned, in a van that looked like the club car on a transcontinental streamliner. Mrs. Cugat had seen them go from a crouching position under a lilac bush. She stretched and yawned now, and then went into the bathroom to draw a bath. When Mr. Cugat came in an hour later, she was dozing across the foot of the bed.

'Oh hello, you back?' she said, and sat up eagerly.

'Back again,' said Mr. Cugat, whistling cheerily. 'Where you been? Cory said you weren't ——'

'Tell me *all* about it!' Mrs. Cugat interrupted.

'Liz!' expostulated Mr. Cugat, scandalized.

'Oh — I mean did you find the place all right? And did you and Cory get "Precious" safely unloaded and so forth?'

'Sure,' he said. 'We didn't have to do a thing; there was a fella there waiting for us who was very handy getting her out.'

'What'd he look like?' Mrs. Cugat asked breathlessly.

'Sort of half-witted. One side of his face all squinted up.'

Mrs. Cugat had hopped off the bed. 'Come on

and pack, George. I think you and I better be getting out of here.'

'Getting out — why?'

'I think Cory's engagement is about to be broken.'

'What on earth are you talking about?'

'Claiborne's going to get mad at him this time — he's just taken "Beautiful" to be bred to a jackass!'

'What?'

'Accidentally, of course — but she'll never believe it.'

'What do you mean?'

' "Jackass on a mare gets a mule," ' recited Mrs. Cugat glibly, 'and you took "Lovely-Lovely" where a jackass lives.'

'We did not!' Mr. Cugat protested. 'We went to the place they told us — right up the road, big trees, white gate, green mailbox, looked like a fox's hole, and the man was expecting us.'

'I know,' said Mrs. Cugat, piling clothes into her suitcase. 'I was up there this morning, paid him a thirty-dollar stud fee and told him Lady Satin was on the way — then I went out and painted his mailbox green. Get going, darling — we've got to hurry.'

'Ah,' exclaimed Mrs. Cugat, from behind the evening paper, ten days later and safe at home, 'here we are! "Sailing tonight aboard the S.S.

Mariposa for an extended cruise of the South Seas will be Mr. Cory Cartwright of this city. Mr. Cartwright plans to spend some time on the island of Bali. Accompanying him is his great-aunt, Miss Lydia Bonbright of Four Forks, Iowa." — Darling, it worked!'

Mr. Cugat raised his eyes. 'Have you thought how we'll look in sarongs?' he asked gravely.

. . . to have and to hold . . .

WHEN the Cugats were in Bermuda, Mrs. Cugat, on her bicycle, spun around a corner and ran smack into Gary Cooper — which led, following one of Destiny's capricious patterns, to a new hat — for Mr. Cugat.

Gary Cooper had risen, dusted himself off, smiled (a little grimly) at Mrs. Cugat, and silently limped away. Mrs. Cugat had picked up her bicycle, smiled back, and pedaled on bedazzled. Around the next corner she had run smack into Mr. Cugat.

'Good Lord, darling, you're a menace on that thing!' he'd said, amiably extricating himself and an armload of tennis racquets. 'What have you been doing? — you're all pink.' So she'd told him, a little breathlessly, spangling the account with bright particulars and suppositions, but all the while, with a divergent piece of her mind, marking him in a brand-new light. Gary Cooper had looked

like a picture in *Esquire* of a man in Bermuda. What did Mr. Cugat look like? Nothing on earth but himself, in Bermuda — or at home — or in New York — or on the road to Mandalay or the bonny braes of Doon. Seeking the key to this triumph of personality over surroundings, however colorful, she'd gone over him carefully with covert little glances as he walked jauntily along beside her, swishing his racquets, and found her answer — that hat.

Gary Cooper's hat had been low of crown, flaring of brim, featherweight, pale gray — a pork-pie; under it his face had looked as brown as a buckeye, his eyes as blue as the sea. She'd glanced again at Mr. Cugat's hat, straight upon his brow, dark and undistinguished — it was as seasoned as an old boot.

It looked, in fact, as if it grew there, a part of Mr. Cugat himself, rather than a mere appurtenance designed to enhance. And it was the only hat he'd brought with him. There were others at home on his closet shelf — three or four, anyway — but they all were exactly the same — except that some were, possibly, darker. Mr. Cugat ordered them at intervals, expensively made to order, and he wore them in a mysterious rotation, known only to himself. She couldn't remember that he'd ever thrown one away. He was like that: once something which belonged to him had proved its worth it became cherished. She loved new things, clothes in particular, because they were new, and when they were old she cast them off. But Mr. Cugat took new things strictly on probation. Once having accepted something, however, it was seldom relinquished. That droopy Burberry he'd bought in London on their wedding trip, that beloved, too-long sweater he played golf in, those too-short flannels he played tennis in — he'd worn them for years! And when some treasure did finally fall into disuse through age or accident, he was likely to try to replace it with the nearest thing to it he could possibly find. All of which, she'd concluded irritably, considering Gary Cooper again, was just perfectly ridiculous.

The upshot had been that after lunch, somehow emboldened by the Cooper collision, she had simply gone out, while Mr. Cugat napped in innocence, bought him a gray pork-pie at the English Sport Shop for two pounds, ten and six, and carried it home to him.

Presented with misgivings and received with suspicion, it had been a howling success. It was soft of color, and shady of brim, and it had, in quite a different way, become Mr. Cugat quite as much as Gary Cooper. Two men, whom Mr. Cugat considered sound, had asked where he'd got it. Walking around the town, people had given him quick second glances: beneath its paleness, his face had appeared dark, interesting, his eyes light and clear. He'd looked leisurely, urbane — a part of the scene, no creature of quick vacations. Mrs. Cugat had thrilled with pride — it was like being with someone else. Mr. Cugat, imperturbable throughout and, to the casual eye at least, unaware of his change of spots, had, however, gone out and bought himself three new bow ties. His old fedora remained on the closet shelf for the rest of their stay — a period tinged for Mrs. Cugat with the sweet unfamiliarity of a honeymoon.

She thought of all this now as, Bermuda behind, the *President Roosevelt* chopped through cold seas on the last night of the homeward voyage and she struggled with packing in a pitching stateroom. Mr. Cugat's dark suit and heavy overcoat swung in readiness in the wardrobe. His stiff collar, with the tie inserted, clean handkerchief and gloves reposed waiting on the dressing-table. Having thus selected his debarkation costume, he had retired to the bar, 'to be out of your way,' he'd said. Over on top of his open trunk reposed the pork-pie and the fedora in unfortunate approximation — the fedora looking more stodgy than ever. Bearing her last piece of tissue paper, she clambered over the intervening boxes and bags and packed the pork-pie tenderly away, slinging the fedora across the room to Mr. Cugat's bed. What a pity he had to descend to it again. Butterfly back into grub.

Off and on during the next hour she eyed it, sitting there, shapeless, dark and mellow on the white spread — it wasn't even a becoming hat, she thought with distaste. If Mr. Cugat, now that he had escaped its hold, could only be prevailed upon to buy himself a new one in New York — a town counterpart of the pork-pie — something with a little dash! But knowing Mr. Cugat, she knew that as long as he had what he considered a perfectly good hat it was not likely that he would go buying himself another for any such frivolous reason as dash. Or even that his own wife was considering him a grub. As long as he had a perfectly good hat he'd wear it until it rotted. As long as he had a perfectly good hat. What if he didn't have a perfectly good

hat? What if he didn't have any hat? *Then* he'd have to buy a new one. Mrs. Cugat stood transfixed in the center of the cabin, her eyes on the fedora. Determination, consummate and crazy, seized her; grabbing it, she marched across the room, wrenched open the porthole and poked Mr. Cugat's perfectly good hat through.

Reaction, of course, set in cruelly. Lashed by guilt, she remained wide-eyed most of the night. The ship creaked and throbbed and her mind raced unbridled through the dark. Mr. Cugat had always been the gentlest of men, but perhaps he had never been driven, quite, to rage. What would he say to her if, somehow, he discovered she had thrown his hat overboard? What would he do? What would he think? She couldn't imagine. She hardly knew what to think herself. She must have been temporarily insane. She curled down into her bed in panic, with an absurd desire to pull the covers over her head — then she reached up and turned on the light. Mr. Cugat, across the way, was cuddled into his pillow wearing a trustful expression. She averted her eyes and got up for the aspirin.

The morning, however — perhaps the aspirin — brought new strength of purpose. Leaning against the rail, she watched the lettered piers slide by and managed brave and imperturbable talk with two people from Baltimore.

'Where is Mr. Cugat?' they said, and she replied steadily, 'Looking for his hat — it's been mislaid.'

'His hat! How odd!' — 'Are you sure you didn't pack it?' — 'Perhaps he left it in the smoking-room last night — we saw him there. Ronald, Mr. Cugat was wearing a hat when he came into the smoking-room last night, wasn't he? Surely he was! Wasn't it one of those Tyrolean ones with a feather? — I seem to remember his putting it down on a table. Go see, Ronald, the steward will know ——'

Mrs. Cugat, suppressing a mad picture of Mr. Cugat in a green Tyrolean with a feather (was he leading some kind of double life?), restrained Ronald of Baltimore. 'Really,' she said, 'don't bother, *please!* Mr. Cugat is doing everything necessary ——'

Mr. Cugat, just then, his coat collar turned up and his hair spiked by the wind, went by, officially accompanied by two heavily braided ship's officers. He was obviously doing everything possible. He tossed her a wry grimace of resignation in passing, and the knife in her heart turned.

She didn't see him again until they were about to dock; this time, cold and even more disheveled, hurrying up to the bridge. 'Meet me in C,' he called. 'You get a customs man.' The people from Baltimore continued perturbed and anxious to help, but their name began with M, so they were mercifully deflected, leaving her to proceed on alone.

Standing in C, with a welcoming grin, was Cory Cartwright, friend of Mr. Cugat's bosom. He was accompanied by a woman in Russian boots and a man with four Bedlington terriers.

'Liz, old girl!' he cried, embracing her warmly, 'you look shot to hell — these are the Fishleighs — where's George?'

'He'll be along,' said Mrs. Cugat, hastily summoning presence to match the Fishleighs'. 'He's mislaid his hat. What a surprise, Cory. I didn't know you were in New York!'

'I came down on bank business for George. He's been trying to lay hands on Fishleigh, here, for over a year, but he's a slippery devil, aren't you, boy? — always abroad. I was so proud of finally nailing

him while George was away that I brought him
down to the boat to show him off.'

'Was the trip hideous?' inquired Mrs. Fishleigh
pleasantly. 'Nobody on board, I suppose.'

'How about a drink?' said Mr. Fishleigh.

'I'm afraid we'll have to stop and pick up a hat
for George first,' said Mrs. Cugat, thinking with
sudden pleasure of Mr. Cugat's old fedora tossing
somewhere off Sandy Hook.

'Here comes George now,' Cory said suddenly.
'He's got a hat.' Mrs. Cugat swung around —
Mr. Cugat was threading his way through the
crowd looking nonchalant and serene. On his head,
appearing peculiarly rustic in combination with his
full-skirted, long, dark overcoat, was his pork-pie,
pale and flaring.

'That hat was never mislaid,' muttered Cory.
'Some good friend just hid it.'

How on earth had he found his trunk!

Mr. Cugat came up wreathed in smiles and
greeted the Fishleighs with enthusiasm; he looked
like a visiting planter — pre-Civil War. 'Cripes,'
he murmured, in an aside to Cory, 'this *is* a welcome
home! If we can just separate the old boy from
those lambs and get him down to the bank, we can
clean up the Fish Trust for good and all.'

'That was my idea,' Cory muttered. 'I haven't
let him out of my sight for three days.'

'How about a drink?' said Mr. Fishleigh.

'I'll take bromo,' said Cory wearily.

'I'll go up to the hotel with Liz and meet you at the bank in an hour,' said Mr. Cugat, aloud. And so, after attending to the baggage, Mrs. Fishleigh, the Cugats, and the Bedlingtons set out in the Fishleigh town car and Cory, relief in sight, steered Mr. Fishleigh firmly into a taxi. During the ride Mrs. Cugat sat silent and tried not to look at Mr. Cugat any oftener than she had to. Mrs. Fishleigh, however — probably a jaded collector of the unique — appeared captivated. What was worrying Mrs. Cugat, however, was not this. A horrid little fear clutched at her heart.

'You're going to stop on your way downtown and pick up another hat, aren't you?' she ventured, and crossed her fingers, as, finally settled in their hotel, Mr. Cugat prepared to depart for Wall Street.

'This one will do me all right till I get home,' he replied easily, busy with his briefcase.

'George! you can't go around wearing that hat in New York, it's almost white — you look like a cowboy or something.'

Moved by the agony in her voice, Mr. Cugat peered in the mirror. 'I see what you mean,' he grinned, tilting its broad brim rakishly to one side. Then he put it soberly back again. 'But what's the difference? I've got a lot of perfectly good hats at home. We're only going to be here until tomorrow night; I'm certainly not going to buy another hat just for a day and a half.'

'Oh, but darling, you look *awful!* What will people think? I was so embarrassed I almost died just coming up from the boat and into the hotel. I was afraid maybe they'd think we were queer and not even let us in. I saw the man at the desk looking so funny — and think of the Fishleighs ——'

Mr. Cugat snorted derisively. 'The room clerk! Good God! You don't think I'm going to spend good money to impress a bunch of room clerks and doormen, do you? As for the Fishleighs, he'll be blind by afternoon and won't know whether I have a hat on or not, and she can —— I suppose you didn't notice that outfit *she* was wearing!'

'O George, I know' — Mrs. Cugat was close to tears. 'You never care what people think of you. I think it's marvelous to be that way — strong — but I'm not, and I'll simply suffer if I have to go around with you in that thing!'

'Go around with somebody else, then,' said Mr. Cugat shortly. 'I'm about to close a deal that's been worrying us for two years and I can't seem to get very upset, just now, over the shape of my hat. Why don't you call up your stagy friend who was out for the Coronet Ball — I'll bet he wears a wimple.' Whereupon he buckled up his briefcase and departed.

'Well,' she said hopelessly to the closed door. 'I've got only myself to blame.'

That night the Fishleighs entertained lavishly — dinner, the theater, night clubs. The pork-pie, offset by a tuxedo, made Mr. Cugat look like the gambler in an oldtime Western — instead of the planter of the morning or the cowboy of the afternoon — it was amazing, the extent of its repertoire. Mr. Cugat, impervious to gibes, enjoyed himself hugely, but every time they moved on to another place or gave the pork-pie up to a hat-check girl, Mrs. Cugat shrank in shame.

The next morning she tackled him again. 'Darling, if only for my sake, won't you please buy yourself a new hat today?' Mr. Cugat, feeling none too well, stared at her blankly; then it came back to him — apparently but a small iron in yesterday's fire. 'Good grief, Liz,' he exclaimed, 'are you still harping on *that!*'

'Yes, I am,' she said, with sudden spirit. 'It's making me perfectly miserable. I'm so ashamed I could die. It's spoiling the whole trip!'

Mr. Cugat's answer to this was a disgusted silence, which he broke with finality in his tone. 'You're altogether too sensitive,' he said, 'always worrying about the impression you're making. Get this once and for all, I'm *not* going to buy another hat. I don't need another hat. If you're ashamed of me,

pretend you don't know me, but I don't want to
hear any more about it.' Mrs. Cugat turned her
face to the wall.

He had business downtown again, so he arose
without further ado, dressed somewhat shakily, and
got ready to leave. Putting his hat on he caught her
eye in the mirror and winked in a friendly fashion,
then he deliberately turned the pork-pie straight
up in front, which made him look, this time, like a
pirate, and walked out.

Mrs. Cugat, however, was not amused. She lay
for some time savoring injury; then she got up, went
to the phone and called WIckersham 2-3486. This
was the number of that gentleman to whom Mr.
Cugat had imputed the wearing of a wimple. He was
the designer for the stage, whose encounter with the

Cugats at the Coronet Ball had been so ill-starred.
Dashingly costumed as a Riff bandit, he had paid
marked attention to Mrs. Cugat and then accidentally pushed Mr. Cugat downstairs. Mr. Cugat had
been costumed in a suit of armor and had got badly
bent. He was wont to refer to the Riff pertly.
Mrs. Cugat could think of no one, at this point,
whom she'd rather see — or, after the humiliation
of the past twenty-four hours, be seen with, particularly by Mr. Cugat.

The Riff, when she got him on the phone, was
enthusiastic. 'Angel!' he said. 'At last!' Mrs. Cugat
was a little startled at such lovely warmth, but very
pleased. 'You'll have lunch with me,' he said.
Why, yes, she would. 'I've been painting, Baby,
and am filthy — *but* filthy! Can you wait till I
clean up?' She could. 'Orchids, camellias, or
mimosa?' he asked.

Well, this was something like. She put back the
receiver and, whistling softly, went to the mirror to
see if her hair would do. She felt bold, devil-may-
care. What did it matter to her what Mr. Cugat
wore — let him go around in a fireman's hat if he
wanted to.

The Riff had done a nice job of getting cleaned
up, she found when she met him downstairs. He
was almost too splendid — it made her feel mousy.
The orchids, however, when they were produced,

nearly covered her, and helped. They went to 'Twenty-One.' Nothing they had to eat or drink was mentioned on the menu; their fare was entirely made up of rare, nameless specialties known only to the Riff, Charlie, and Jack. The Fishleighs were there with the Bedlingtons, and Mrs. Cugat waved gaily. They even saw Gary Cooper again (needless to say, without his pork-pie), but he did not speak to Mrs. Cugat. Seeing him, however, reminded her of Mr. Cugat's pork-pie, and she freshened her attentions to her host.

After lunch they strolled down Fifth Avenue, Mrs. Cugat feeling gay and worldly and far removed from niggling economies and little quarrels. The Riff said he wanted to show her his work, but she was putting this off, not being entirely sure to what looking at his work might lead. She strongly suspected to no good, and it seemed such a shame to precipitate things. They stopped idly in front of a jeweler's window to admire a chaste display and were reflected in clear mirror — she and the Riff and her orchids. He really was divine-looking — almost too handsome. Then the door spun open and out came Mr. Cugat, looking ridiculous but debonair. Mrs. Cugat caught her breath. What would he do? Get belligerent like last time?

She need not have worried.

'Well, well, it's a small world,' he said, coming

over and grasping the Riff by the hand. 'Fancy seeing you two again.'

Mrs. Cugat sighed softly and tried to forget the pork-pie. Really, he was a darling — never at a loss, certainly.

'What in the world have you been doing in there?' she asked, hunting her voice.

'Well,' said Mr. Cugat, 'I was walking by and noticed this in the window. It looked sort of like you, so I went in and bought it.'

. Mrs. Cugat steadied herself and took the square case he produced from his pocket.

'Jeepers!' said the Riff, as she opened it. It was a pin — iridescent, intricate, an orchid — made all of diamonds and an occasional emerald.

'Cute, isn't it?' said Mr. Cugat. 'Do you like it, Liz? I thought you would because it's a flower ——'

'They took plenty off you for that,' breathed the Riff in undisguised awe.

'Well, yes,' said Mr. Cugat, 'but you always have to pay for workmanship. Look, all the petals move — little hinges. I don't mind paying if I get something, do you?'

Mrs. Cugat stood dumb — emotionally scrambled. Was there anybody quite like Mr. Cugat? No, there was not. Not for anything would he spend ten dollars on a hat he didn't think he needed, but on the same day would he buy a piece of jewelry that must have cost hundreds? Yes, he would — without batting an eye — simply because —— What? Because he could see his money's worth in it? Or was it, just possibly, because he knew he'd hurt her? She'd never know — Mr. Cugat was not one to tell her. *Darling* Mr. Cugat!

'Come on over to the hotel,' he was saying jovially to the Riff. 'Cory's having a bunch of people in for a drink — I'm on my way there now.'

Mrs. Cugat took his arm in a sort of coma. It's just small people like me who worry over little things like clothes, she thought. Never again would she mention Mr. Cugat's pork-pie — not even if he went to bed in it!

As if to spare her this test, a river breeze sucked

suddenly through a crosstown gully, spinning around
them in a wild eddy, and Mr. Cugat's pork-pie
fluttered groggily off his head into the air and then
soared like an eagle. They watched it, frozen, and
gasped in concerted dismay, as, suddenly daft, it
plunged beneath a bus. The problem was over —
just like that. It was brought back with brim off.

Mr. Cugat smoothed his hair down ruefully.
'You two go on,' he said. 'Cory's been waiting —
I'll run over here to Cavanagh's — I've had the
damnedest trouble with hats, this trip!'

Mrs. Cugat parted from him, in love and her
heart light. Poor sweet, she thought, it *was* a shame,
after all — he'd looked so jaunty and pleased with
himself when he'd emerged from the jeweler's.
What difference did it make what he wore? — he
was ever himself, regardless.

She felt grateful to Fate, however, when she saw
Cory's bunch of people. They were very varnished;
the Riff fitted in like a piece of their own puzzle.
She related, in an aside to Cory, the pork-pie's fate
and showed him the pin.

'Well,' he said relievedly, 'it looks like maybe you
will live happily ever after. I got a little worried
when I saw fancy-pants, here.'

'Cory,' said Mrs. Cugat. 'Look!'

They were standing in the entryway of the suite,
and toward them down the hall came Mr. Cugat
briskly.

On his head was another gray pork-pie!

'I couldn't help it, Liz,' he explained hurriedly. 'They didn't have any of my kind made up; and anyway, you know, I've got three or four perfectly good ones at home — but they did have this! See, just like the other. I was almost afraid I'd have to send to England for one — darned lucky. You don't *really* mind, do you?'

'No, not really,' she said, smothering frantic laughter.

Cory came forward with introductions. 'The Farquharsons, the Middletons, the Zinks,' he said, and then turned and murmured to a very varnished lady at his side: 'Cugat's from Australia, m'dear. Big kangaroo man and filthy rich. He raises them for the market.'

The lady looked at Mr. Cugat in no surprise. 'I want him,' she said.

Mrs. Cugat tapped gently on Cory's arm. 'Me too,' she said firmly.

THE END